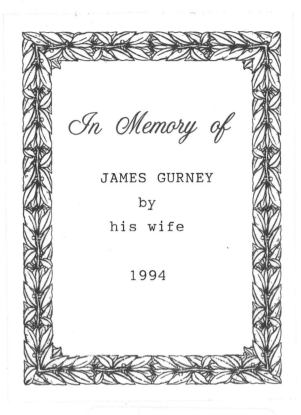

In Memory of

JAMES GURNEY
by
his wife

1994

MF   42603
BARTHELME, PETER

AUTHOR
BRAIN FADE

TITLE

DATE DUE   BORROWER'S NAME

MF   42603
BAPTHELME, PETER

BRAIN FADE

DATE DUE

Previous novels by Peter Barthelme

Tart, with a Silken Finish
Push, Meet Shove

BRAINFADE

PETER BARTHELME

ST. MARTIN'S PRESS / NEW YORK

Library of Congress Cataloging-in-Publication Data

Barthelme, Peter.
        Brainfade / Peter Barthelme.
                p.   cm.
        ISBN 0-312-02879-2
        I. Title.
    PS3552.A7633B73 1989
    813'.54—dc19   89-4083

First Edition

10 9 8 7 6 5 4 3 2 1

For Cynthia P.

BRAINFADE

I COULDN'T GET MY MIND around Dr.
Stone's voice. I expected a booming, positive, I-have-all-
the-answers tone from her, all six feet of her, maybe a gut-
tural snarl to go with her absurdly short fair hair, shorter
than mine, what was left of it.

Instead, I heard a shy little girl's delivery, hesitant in
spots, almost begging for agreement. Half her sentences
ended with an up inflection, like a question, which was
annoying, although looking at her I was inclined toward
patience. Actually, if I didn't like it, the lady looked perfectly capable of twisting my arm until I did.

Surely she was more forceful in shrink-mode?

She was the first woman I had met since I "retired"
whom I wanted. Instantly, even violently, no niceties
needed, I flat wanted her. An amused glint in her grayish

or greenish eyes told me she knew it, too. Or maybe it was the shrink *schtick*, the feeling that she knew, training and experience, the depravities that lie behind our most carefully cultivated façade. Nifty train of thought in a psychiatric clinic, right?

She was looking at me expectantly. I decided I was a little afraid of her. She really couldn't read my mind.

"I'm glad you don't expect perfection," I said. "Mine is not an exact science." Where to look? I met her eyes, drifted down to her body, jerked away, settled on my own hands. Rather large beat-up–looking hands, eight fingers only, teach me to get tangled up in the leader wire when wrestling with angry sharks. I looked back at her.

"More art, actually, especially as you practice it?" She smiled an understanding shrink-smile, eyes alight and curious. She snubbed out her third cigarette. I like doctors with bad habits. Should I mention cancer of the throat?

I made what I thought was a moue. Maybe that would impress her. Maybe if I leaped across the desk and ripped off her white doctor coat. Removing a brassiere not required since none was in evidence. She smiled at me, strong hands cupping her smooth chin. Her features were close to coarse, but she made it work. The sort of woman who was used to stopping traffic. If I claimed temporary insanity, they could lock me up in one of the closed wards right away. Efficient. Her handshake was strong and the fine hair on her arms rippled over muscle, female muscle, long and sleek.

Overpowering woman. Maybe that's why I fantasized. Maybe it was the environment. After all, what better place than a psychiatric clinic? One of the few individually owned such facilities, she had said. The walls had heard generations of sick desires, twisted thoughts, irrational impulses. Too cheerful, too bright, too clean, too much carefully matched blue and gray. Psychologically muted environments to straighten heads. Profits through pain relief. Think of the nerve and drive, the hard assumption of rightness, that had let her, forced her, to create it. Monuments and monument-builders frighten me. I shifted uneasily. New business! screamed my dormant money nerve.

"Tell me again, what you have in mind?"

"I have here, Mr. Beaumont, a two hundred and eight–bed clinic. Each of those beds represents . . . roughly five thousand a week. In revenue? Each *empty* bed therefore represents a loss of that amount, each week. This is . . . bothersome?" Doctors aren't supposed to have a bottom-line approach but maybe that's unfair.

"And I'm to fill the beds with a marketing program?" We used to simply call it advertising but that was *too* simple and not MBA-ish enough. Like comptrollers for head accountant.

"More precisely, you are . . . how do you say it? . . . to make the phones ring? Off the wall?"

"You heard of me." I was stalling.

"Your work is your *curriculum vitae,* Mr. Beaumont." I waved the "Mr." away with my hand.

"And you can treat my lady's problem as part of the deal, Dr. Stone?" I had explained about Tammy early on.

"You would receive the same privileges as any employee . . . not that you would be considered an employee, more a professional, an outside counsel?"

"Hell, I'm just a flack."

"Our budget," she said, peeking at some papers on the desk, "is considerable. At least it *seems* considerable. Although I am far from expert in these matters. Fifty thousand a month?"

"Ten beds," I said. Fifty thousand? Ad agency people figure commissions automatically. Fifteen percent of fifty thousand would be a seventy-five-hundred-dollar feather in my cap. Looked real good against my monthly nut, now hovering at the thousand-dollar mark. I was suddenly ashamed of my currently meager ambitions and achieve-

4 · PETER BARTHELME

ments. Her office, the whole clinic, was a far cry from my burlap-covered plywood furnishings. Blues and grays, no steel desks, almost oppressively cheerful.

"Actually, we could think of it . . . that way. Ten beds full."

She breathed happily and her chest danced a slow dance, dip and sway. Damn, she was wonderful. Imagine all the delightful deviations a full-fledged psychiatrist, Johns Hopkins 1973, would know. I dwelled upon the thought.

She was explaining something, how the clinic format freed her from tiresome hospital rules and regs, experimental modalities, cost efficiencies, and I was thinking whips and chains. A stray ray of light glowed on the fine down on her cheek.

A man-thing barged in and dropped papers on her desk, moving its mouth in what I supposed was a smile. She seemed unperturbed and introduced him as "Horce," her private assistant. He was malformed somehow, nearly as wide as he was tall, and had brown front teeth. Massive forearms and hands, black tufts of hair in the ears and nose, monster hands. He placed one of these mitts on my shoulder to forestall me getting up and squeezed painfully. Odd, intimate contact inside of thirty seconds. I twisted away and ignored his bone-crushing grip. She nodded and he left with a final squeeze of my shoulder muscles, too hard. He had a semilimp, a slight dragging of the left leg. Starched white shirt stretched to contain his shoulders. Squatty legs in jeans. Running shoes.

"Horce was a most destructive individual," she said. "We have managed to channel his impulses into more productive directions."

"He's a doll. You could always use him to frighten the children."

"Or the adults, is it not so?" She lighted another cigarette, Winston, woman had a death wish, and I found *that* erotic, too, and got my tail out of there.

*   *   *

I was perfectly happy as a full-service ad agency in the small town of Victoria, Texas, doing furniture store ads and press releases. A radio spot was a rare and wondrous thing and sixty seconds cost 22 bucks morning or evening drive-times. Okay, it wasn't as exciting or lucrative as my previous agency in Houston, but I enjoyed the small-town pace and characters. I also enjoyed doing my part to repel the fish invasion expected at any minute at Point Lookout, living at my bay cabin, forty minutes from "town." The bay house and the Victoria office were the not-so-shattered remains of my worldly empire, which I had given up almost voluntarily. And lo! how the mighty have fallen, but nobody was trying to kill me currently.

Since I always wore just jeans and a shirt anyhow, my attire fit nicely into Victoria's style, and since I was at the point where I might have fewer years ahead of me than behind me, the few advertisers around figured I knew something. I couldn't talk country no matter how I tried though.

I didn't get bored, as I had feared, and I still took the same pleasure wiping the condensation off my twenty-five-foot Grady-White boat in the still and expectant gray light before dawn. My heart still jumped and thumped when a kingfish whacked one of the trolled baits offshore or when the red-and-white popping cork tilted and slid under the surface as a redfish took my mullet bait.

I didn't quite fit in at the township of Point Lookout and the business community of Victoria, but I didn't quite fit in anywhere. Never had.

My Tammy started out in the key of wonderful, living there with me without the benefit of matrimony or parental approval, until she weirded-out completely and refused to eat. I should have known something was coming when her previous demonstrative nature changed in a bleak cold winter. We started arguing and she couldn't make up her mind what she wanted. I had a strong feeling one six-two Beaumont, fallen ad hero and ace fisherperson, wasn't it. But I never figured she would go bonkers. And I certainly offered, time and again, to take her back to the big city and help her start over. Even without me. Ladies' Choice, all the dances.

We were stuck with each other, better friends than lovers, an impulsive mutual decision transformed into a habit, glued by inertia and the fear of change.

I never figured she'd become food obsessive. Typically, knowing I was being typical, I was understanding-and-patient, then angry, then guilty, then angry again. I think I hit "reasonable" in there a couple of times, too. But she wouldn't, didn't eat, although she seemed to think of nothing but food, weighing and measuring, figuring fractions of an ounce on a pocket calculator. If she had been my child rather than my lover, I might have tried to force-feed her, a disaster for sure. I didn't ask for this, I'd scream mentally and feel ashamed.

To watch a healthy twenty-nine-year-old shrink from a ripely curved 122 pounds down to a nervous and bitchy 100 pounds or so, with no respite in sight, would make anybody nervous. Her periods stopped, she told me somberly and not for any pregnancy reason. Even her funny, spiky punk hairdo wilted.

All she had to do was eat, no matter what distorted vision she saw in the mirror. Scary.

I spent a lot of time out in the boat, kicking my metaphoric ass around. No matter that she had insisted on moving in, an ignored fishing village with sixty or so permanent residents, most of them well over twice her age and with a variety of tobacco-stained teeth, was no place for a lively lady, age too young for me. I should have known better. My approach *must* be wrong. I was over my head. I should be more: caring, sensitive, empathetic. Have a chicken-fried steak, for Christ's sake. Sometimes she said she didn't want to leave, she was happy, let her alone. Often she said let her alone.

My old friend Vince, king of the topless bars, who had brought Tammy on her first time in Point Lookout, had been shocked on his last visit. For a man who was born on concrete, raised on concrete, and lived on concrete, he had taken to wadefishing with a passion. He had all the stuff, stringer, cap, wadefishing belt, custom rods, and shiny reels; but he looked like an elegant blond bouncer even waist deep in salt water.

I had thought the surly sunbitch was going to bat me around, shades of our high school beer-drinking days, until I persuaded him it was not my doing, that I was as frantic as he and didn't have the faintest idea what to do about her. Finally he helped me worry in fine fatherly fashion, which was a switch for a guy who made his living as owner, head-exploiter, of one of Houston's finer topless establishments. A "gentleman's club" said the billboard I did for him.

Anorexia. Nice-sounding word. Fucked disease.

That's one of the major reasons I had obeyed the summons to drive the two hours to Houston and interview the good doctor Stone. The fact that she inspired instant lust within my aging breast and promised to give me an ad budget approximately four times my present total volume was a bonus.

I had not known she was a lady doctor when I picked my best pair of blue jeans and a sorta-silk sports coat to wear on the interview. Especially a lady doctor who could damn near look me in the eye in flat heels and was shaped like an oversize, heroic-scale Penthouse Pet. Unknowing, I had shined my one pair of real shoes, too.

Had I known the budget numbers, I might have bought a tie.

You think you've got your life in order, got it figured out, can settle down a little, moving right along. Then a grinning something comes along and deposits trouble on your head with a wet smack. Anorexia.

Stick with what you know.

I'd make Dr. Stone some fine ads indeed and her troops would poke around in Tammy's brain cells a bit. When we got leveled off, we could pick a sensible direction for us both, no external pressure/guilt to cloud our judgments. Damn, she was a fine-looking, tasty, challenging woman.

Tammy, too, when well.

2

I STAYED ON U.S. 59, the main route south to the Valley from Houston, on the way home and went to the office. Unending flat prairieland, studded with pumpjacks for the wells and growing a little cotton, a little corn, a little soybean. Edna, Louise, Hillje, girl's names for tiny towns. The office was a refuge, but how do you tell your infrequent lover that you're putting her in the funny farm because she won't—can't—eat and you're afraid she's going to die on you?

Dr. Stone would, no doubt, frown on my flippancy.

I was semi-conversant with shrinks and the terminology and the struggles for respectability, scientific respectability, that the entire mental health profession was waging. I had been there and Dr. Hector Edfelter, who had wrestled with me to hold my personal demons at bay, was a dear and much respected person in my private hall of fame. No psy-chopharmacological, multimodality, cross-discipline bull-shit there. Just two guys in a room, struggling. And he was the tougher, if only because he was detached.

So I knew firsthand what could be accomplished if your head was screwed on a touch crooked, when you were willing to work and could stand to look at yourself in a clear mirror. Knew what one trained person could help you accomplish.

Mostly, however, I was saturated with some of the pop-psych and self-help stuff, which was, in my jaundiced old opinion, pap. I wasn't any too fond of some of the reedy, tweedy psych-types I ran across occasionally, for that mat-ter, the ones with strange initials behind their names. I think a master's degree is nice, but never felt compelled to put it on a business card.

"After all," I said to Bullit, A Dog, having rescued her from the nice lawyer down the hall, who was her adopted second owner, "if everything was supposed to be shared and loving, why do they put doors on bathrooms?" She wagged her scuffy tail and looked expectantly at the cache of Milk Bones, trying to point out *she* loved me without reservation and would be happy to eat anytime. Bullit never talked back.

Dutifully I called the Evanses, the closest phone in Point Lookout and the people who had semi-raised me when I came, full grown, to the fishing village. I told "the wife" that I would be late and would she tell Tammy?

"Beaumont, we've got to *do* something about her!"

"I'm—"

"I invited her for dinner, chicken and mashed potatoes, all the stuff she likes, told her we'd just give her *tiny* por-tions and wouldn't fuss and I swear she was crying when she left."

"She can't help—"

"I know that. You remember that singer-girl, she *died*!"

"Well, Tammy's not quite—"

"It's getting bad. Real bad."

"I know it," I said simply.

"Well, you'd better do something because I can't stand to see her waste away."

"Yes-um." I finally got off the phone, not feeling hungry myself suddenly, and knew she was right. Maybe Dr. Stone could offer some answers, although I gathered that eating disorders were not her specialty. "Marriage and relationship problems," she had said in a cloud of Winston-smoke.

"But knowing the boss-lady can't hurt," I told Bullit.

Dr. Stone had loaded me up with enough competitive hospital ads and brochures to choke a goat. I dutifully waded through quite a number. About an hour into this task, I was convinced that they all were written by a young woman who was raised in a Skinner box and had spent her adolescent and young-adult years behind a similar protective shield.

My mythical copywriter never had a pimple on her perky nose, never got stood up, had a delightful and multi-orgasmic sexual life with a systems engineer who was sensitive and caring and ranked eighteenth on the pro tennis tour. Her work was rewarding and challenging and her relationship with Mommy and Daddy was just super. Did I mention she did charity work?

I hated her instinctively.

What they were selling was not the world I lived in. The promises, implied or baldly stated, were unrealistic and the tenor of the copy was not going to be meaningful to a drunk who checked the fenders every morning for bloodstains or the kid who planned to sexually assault his teacher. Or the Tammy, who was not-eating herself into the grave. Sharing. Sensate focus. Skewed reactions. Assimilation of erroneous data. Bullshit.

I was pissed and took it out on my faithful typewriter.

When I wanted to really pound the keys, I ignored the computer and used the Selectric and wished for my old manual typewriter, which could wince.

"YOU'RE A DRUNK," said the first headline. "WANT TO MAKE SOMETHING OF IT?"

I didn't neglect other abused substances. My cocaine addiction ad read "YOU'RE STICKING YOUR FUTURE UP YOUR NOSE."

After this I began to be slightly hostile. But when I was through, about two hours' worth of two-finger pounding on the IBM, I had a set of print ads that would adapt nicely to radio (the fifty grand wasn't really enough for television in the country's fourth largest market, not if we were to have any print ads at all) and a solid start on a sales brochure.

No pretty country-club pictures either. My visuals were candid, Diane Arbus–type photos of real people doing real-people disgusting things. Zip on the sharing.

Even weird Dr. Stone will probably find these too tough to stomach, I thought. But they're right on. She was a pistol, was Dr. Stone.

With that happy thought, I collected Bullit and hit the highway for home.

God, she looked bad.

Tammy, when she had the misfortune to get a good job as my secretary/assistant in another lifetime, was a curvy, bouncy, near-beautiful girl-next-door type. With a sharp brain and a cutting/funny tongue in her golden head. And an inexplicable fondness for an old fart like me.

Now she looked thirty-five going on sixty and bony. Drawn features and hollow eyes and her once-proud breasts were little skin flaps hanging on her chest. No energy, of course, no fuel. She was too tired to come to work these days, although when we started she could wear me down, no problem.

I coaxed a little soup down her, told her about the new account, and waited while she went away to throw up the soup. She ran the shower to disguise the noise of her up-chucking but I had caught her at it too many times.

I didn't pretend to know what twist in brainwaves told her that her emaciated body was grossly fat, but that's what she saw in the mirror and believed. Told me so when we could still talk a little. Maybe no other person is really your responsibility, aside from your infants, but you'd have a hard time convincing me of that. I *had* to do something. Guilt alone.

So when she came back, hesitant and apologetic and a little fearful, Bullit whining off to the side, I said, "And you're going with me."

"Back to Houston?"

"Actually it's outside of Houston, down toward Galveston Bay. It's a hospital, no, a private clinic, informal, and I want you to admit yourself."

"For what?" she asked, and I wanted to roar at her.

"For a general checkup and a look at our disagreement about your eating."

"We don't *have* any disagreement, you are pushing me *again* and I *told* you . . ."

I held up both hands to stop the familiar litany. "Okay, okay. No argument needed. But I want you to do this. The doctors and therapists can look at you with unprejudiced eyes, and you can convince them, okay?"

"They'll probably put me on a diet." She pouted unbecomingly.

"Possibly. But let's let them decide."

And, after an hour or so of debate, we left it there. I felt a sense of achievement. Maybe just a shifting of responsibility. But Mrs. Evans was right. We had to *do* something.

In the literature I had scanned as research for my ads, the concept of family therapy appeared again and again, the idea that the family environment could be one of the causes of whatever problem was giving trouble. What they didn't mention is the frustration of dealing with someone else's nonbiological illness, the anger you had to repress, like my desire to solve the problem with a double helping of mashed potatoes. Maybe they got to it in family group. I suppressed a few gallons of this and hugged-up on Tammy, getting a familiar jolt of fear because she was so frail.

She went to bed and I sat up and felt hollow and scared. Tammy was compulsive about cleaning too and I was careful not to make a mess. I liked the Marine barracks motif, actually. But that was as far as my aberration went, no danger of eating disorders, not for a man who fantasized about peanut butter and bacon sandwiches frequently.

3

I DIDN'T LIKE THE way they treated Tammy at the clinic. On the other hand, they agreed to my ads and media plan without a murmur and paid in advance, with a check that probably would shock my banker. That was fairly easy to take. The stuff *was* good. I was not accustomed to people who apparently appreciated good. Dr. Stone ran the meeting offhandedly, only smoker at the conference table, but everybody watched her before they voiced an opinion. Maybe I could sell the campaigns to similar clinics in seven states. Hi Ho Greed, away!

Tammy hadn't fussed too much, answered questions, helped me fill out the forms. Maybe a token protest, maybe she was sparing my pride. A touch of reason creeping in? Maybe she just wanted out and away. Great thought,

Beaumont, here I was being benevolent and maybe she wanted out.

I had made arrangements to place the ads, if approved, in advance so most of my initial work was done. The sales brochure remained but the media was under control. Hanging around a town and a business for a decade or two has certain virtues. One was that a dear friend, who now was the sales manager of the biggest country station in town, had listened to my pleas and pulled station rankers for all radio stations on her computer. Yes, I know that media ratings are inherently inaccurate but they beat the hell out of guesswork. And there's something comforting in a printout that says that X dollars will give you a "reach" of 328,000 women age twenty-five-to-thirty-four with a frequency of 3.2. Impressed me, and I *knew* it was only a guide.

They had practically shanghaied Tammy. An initial "consultation," a grave shake of the head to me, insurance papers signed and forwarded, and my lover was in the hospital and I couldn't visit for a week. I think she was my lover, I hadn't had the opportunity to check for a while.

There were a lot of locked doors in the clinic.

"We'll have a course of treatment outlined and a prognosis soon," the nurse said brusquely, banging on her computer terminal, which was connected to their own mainframe. What was the basic overhead here? I wondered. Need a helluva lot of raw material, the patients, to process just to keep the doors open.

My sputtering questions and demands for an explanation met with an oh-so-patient sigh and a poorly written pamphlet that told me that "anorexia is a puzzling and difficult disease." I already knew that.

When they took her away, papers signed and insurance verified, forms all filled out, I had the scary/excited feeling you get waving the kids off on the bus to camp. Free at last, free at last, ohmigod.

I wandered a bit, getting the feel of this busy place, something I probably should have done before writing the ads. Everybody busy, everybody superficially friendly in a hello-don't-bother-me-while-I'm-about-this-serious-business sort of way. Wings and doors and signs. Unused recreational facilities, net sagging on the courtyard badminton court.

I headed outside to the truck, glad I had left the windows down. I wouldn't be able to grip the steering wheel if I left it locked and baking under the sun. I swung up and in and a hand tapped me on the shoulder.

The back of my head whacked the window frame and I was snarling and fist-clenched ready until I saw it was just a kid, seventeen—eighteen, big and gawky, complete with pimples.

"Sorry, mister, need a ride into town." His eyes wouldn't look at me and the door opened on the other side and he flinched. Good ol' Horce leaned in, smiling. Before I could get organized, the kid was lifted out without effort, Horce chiding him gently and shaking his body, kid's head snapping back and forth.

"Take it easy," I shouted.

"Second time Davy's run away," Horce crooned. "Shouldn't do that, Dr. Stone doesn't like it, shouldn't do that."

By the time I got out and around the Blazer, Horce was halfway back into the hospital with his burden, still shaking the poor kid, who offered no resistance although he was six inches taller than his captor. Not my affair, I suppose. Kid was probably a troubled kid. Have to face reality sometime.

I didn't like it, not at all. But what to do? I got back in and started up, letting the A/C blast away at the heat. Poor kid. Hope they got him straightened out; keep him away from Horce for starters. I headed for Houston.

*   *   *

Since I apparently had no Tammy obligations, I went to Vince's place, driving I-45 into Houston and hoping for an invitation to spend the night with my old friend. You can too go home again. It was the same dark and nearly tasteful topless club with the obligatory phallic bar in the middle of the stage and ladies feigning delightful fits of abandon. I settled in with a bourbon, perfectly prepared to letch. He didn't let me check out the current crop of dancers with anywhere near the thoroughness they deserved, instead hustled me back to his private office and demanded Tammy news.

"Well, they think she's anorexic and they think they can do something about it," I told him. "It's a puzzling disease."

"She just won't eat?"

"She still thinks she's fat."

"She's a toothpick!"

"Try and tell her that. She looks in the mirror—like those old distorted funhouse mirrors, that's what she sees. A fat lady, gross."

"It doesn't make sense."

"Where does it say it has to?"

We drank for a while and he told me that AIDS had been good for business, look but not touch, and I asked about a couple of apparently departed dancers and he shrugged.

He was glad for my new business and laughed at my description of Dr. Stone, told me about a girl who used to work for him, billed as "The Amazon," and the funny little fat men who spent big bucks on her.

"She was five-eleven, claimed six-three, and they ate it up."

"Every man needs an Everest."

And he invited me to stay with him for the duration.

Tammy's therapist was a bland fellow with a Hitler moustache who told me he was heading the "treatment team." He also observed that the "antecedents of anorexia are often obscure, rooted in the familial situation." When he got to multimodality, I tuned out. I gathered that he foresaw a long stay.

"As long as the insurance holds up, huh?" I said crudely, and he went on as if I hadn't spoken. Group therapy, individual psychotherapy, a supportive, nonstressful environment was the deal, he said.

When she was brought out to see me, rather like a prize heifer on display, she clung to the guy's arm and told me she was doing fine and that everybody was nice and she was comfortable and didn't need anything.

She seemed anxious to get back to her nonstressful environment and she wouldn't let go of Hitler. Where were the wisecracks and smart-ass? Actually, she seemed anxious to get away from me. And I was the hero.

I went looking for my friend Dr. Stone and was told she was "in a session" and could not be interrupted for any reason. So I waited outside her office and amused myself by attempting to read the journals piled up on the coffee table. In about forty-eleven ways I was doing serious harm to myself and my body, it appeared, not stressing a positive lifestyle as the bedrock problem. Horce came out of her office and nodded at me. If he tried more of that shoulder-squeezing shit, I'd stomp his ugly face. He bustled off.

Dr. Stone's patients had a languorous and unstressed look when they finally emerged, much kissing and hugging, some of it rather more intimate than I thought was required.

The doctor herself beamed at her little group, five couples of young to middle age, and reminded everybody that she'd see them on Thursday. They all would be there, thanks so much, I really felt I got a lot out of this, really nice to be here, glad we could share, and I tried to make six-two of adperson invisible behind *HealthNotes*, while scoping out the females.

I swear they looked almost . . .

She ushered me into her office and told me her professional peers were disturbed.

"And it is entirely your fault, Mr. Beaumont."

"Mine?"

"Your radio ads—spots?—have them all upset. Much too . . . strong medicine sometimes tastes poorly."

"Especially if it works."

"It *is* working, I've had to add another interventionist."

"We used to call them 'closers,'" I remarked. "I want to talk about Tammy."

"She's a dear girl, I think." Dr. Stone settled into her professional pose, hands folded beneath her chin. "We find that the entire spectrum of eating disorders seems to attack people—many females, for some reason—who otherwise seem almost exuberantly healthy."

"What's the prognosis?" Now I was talking jargon.

"The first step is to determine what is the underlying *cause* of the problem. What is . . . awry in the interaction of her conscious and subconscious. What is causing her to have these feelings, which manifest themselves by a distorted self-image. She's a little old . . ." She was doing her weird inflections. I was beginning to like it.

"She's twenty-nine!"

"Oh, not too old for *you*, Mr. Beaumont. I merely mean we see less of this disorder after the early twenties, normally."

I looked at her sharply, not real pleased by her comment, which might have made me feel defensive if I wasn't being careful not to have any but socially appropriate feelings in the shrink's office. You'd think I was the patient here. I needed to keep at least some of my feelings from Dr. Stone.

"It is best that you pull away, during this stage. For the moment . . . let Tammy fixate on other things. You may be the problem, after all."

"I? Why me?"

"Your attraction for her is obvious, but perhaps in some—irrational?—way that is causing her difficulties. Which again are manifest . . . with this problem. Have you undergone therapy, Mr. Beaumont?" Click went the Bic and she blew smoke at me.

"What pertinence does that have?" I was a wee bit pissed.

"None, perhaps, but . . ."

"In any case, I did go under therapy."

"Go under?"

"I spent a lot of hours with Hector Edfelter, working real hard. Do you know him?"

"An excellent physician, I admire him tremendously."

"Thank you. Or, Hector thanks you."

"So . . ."

"What was the group that just left, Dr. Stone?"

"It was my biweekly advanced relationships group. Why do you ask?"

"Because they seemed . . . humid."

"It is a very close and hard-working group and we are probing the limits of individual relationships in a group context. It makes for a high degree of enforced—welcome?—intimacy, and perhaps that is what you observed."

Then she winked at me and I blushed.

Vince was annoyed with me. In fact, we were rapidly rubbing raw the friendship of more than twenty years. Fish and guests began to have an odor after a few days, said my mother. And even though Vince's Southampton home was more than big enough for the two of us, we were getting on each other's nerves.

"Make the bitch tell you!" he'd exploded when I had a noncommittal clinic report.

"It's not that easy."

"First, you have to try. Quit staring at her boobs and try. Try asking maybe."

"Not funny, or true."

"Well, I don't see—"

"Look, Vince, you're perfect at the topless club business, okay? That does not, repeat not, make you a psychology expert. Nor a genius in the field of eating disorders!"

"All I want . . ."

"All *we* want is Tammy well. I've got her in the place I think can make her well. Now get off my back."

"I still say—"

"Please don't. In fact, let's let me hook-em out of here before we both wind up saying a bunch of stuff we don't mean."

He agreed silently and I was glad because I had no desire to get in a violent quarrel with my old friend. Primarily because I secretly believed that he could tear off my head and do something dreadful in the resulting opening if aroused. I was packed and gone in record time, trudging down the 120 miles of U.S. 59 like a defeated child trudging home from the baseball game that his parents forgot.

I mustered all sorts of scintillating arguments even before the notorious speed trap in Kendleton, a mostly black community about forty miles out of Houston. The overeager policemen are collectively known as the "White Knight" on the CBs. That craze had come and gone and some manufacturer somewhere probably had six million of the little radios, carried on the books as unsold inventory. See hula hoops, duration of.

To hell with Vince. I wondered if Dr. Stone was the sort of woman who would bait her own hook.

4

I MANAGED TO GET IN and out of my Point Lookout cabin without having to undergo the interrogation of the Evanses, who were positively parental about Tammy, when they weren't wondering aloud about the chances of our relationship succeeding. I had kept them informed and they were both grateful we were doing something but they had a country skepticism about the entire field of psychiatry.

Me too, come to think of it.

But I slept in my own bed, patted the boat on its trailer in the morning, snuck out early and hit the road for Victoria, the office and my other clients, assuming I had any left.

The answering machine would have complained to the Labor Relations Board if it hadn't been so busy. Its tape was jammed with messages from new best friends of mine. At least that's what one booming voice after another told me they were. Male or female, they boomed.

Media salespeople.

The minute an ad or spot hits the air, if it's not something we all know and love, a tremor goes through the ad business. Minor tremor perhaps, but enough to fill up an hour-long answering machine tape. New spot comes on, eager salesperson hears same, contacts advertiser to discover who placed spot, and calls this new best friend with sincere arguments to show him why the spot should be on "my" station/paper/billboard/skywriting or whatever.

They could devour time. "Thought I'd call to see when it's convenient . . ." or "Wanted to drop by to show you the numbers . . ." or "I know you're busy so I'll just take a few minutes . . ."

Since I had the first flight of media placed, I didn't have to talk to them. I ferreted out the few client calls, indignantly pointed out to the *Victoria Advocate* that I had already paid my bill and had them apologizing for their computer instantly, heard about the reappearance of the tarpon at Pass Cavallo, and looked at the scanty mail. Then I played an abbreviated game of darts against myself and tied my previous 2–5–20–Out record. Tarpon in the pass and no really pressing problems, what a deal! I looked at my bank balance fondly and put the machine back on.

Not a bad morning's work.

And I was still in good favor with my Victoria clients. I saw several of them in the afternoon, fended off their half-jokes about "big time" and took jobs, reported on assignments, straightened out bills, and generally acted like the one-man band I was. The project causing the most troubles was a freebie, 'twas ever thus, an economic development brochure for the town. I solved the problem with the chamber of commerce guy by offering to take more pictures of historic landmark homes and happy people, all ethnic groups. Why I had let them talk me into being the concept man, the writer, the photographer, and chief beggar for free printing, I'll never know. Maybe my good works quotient was down. Maybe I knew they needed it. I bitched about do-gooder stuff and did more of it every year.

The phone rang all afternoon and I let the abused machine handle the rush—no complaints from it yet although I resolved to be careful around toasters and other dangerous appliances for the next few days—monitoring and interrupting when required.

I didn't know there *were* that many media salespersons. Each with the perfect medium for Dr. Stone's clinic. I checked through the paper, noted that there was the barest mention of tarpon in the pass, and had my desk clear shortly after four o'clock.

Just before five, I picked up the phone, ran the gauntlet of receptionist, secretary, and secretary and asked Dr. Stone if she'd ever caught a tarpon and would she like to start now?

5

THE TARPON IS A peculiar fish, one
that has resisted most of the fish scientists' efforts to cate-
gorize it, examine it, determine its habits, rank it, and generally put it in its place.

I like that in a fish.

The Texas coast was once a noted hotspot for tarpon
fishing, Port Aransas and the mouth of the Colorado River
at Freeport two of the best-known spots. Franklin Roosevelt came to Port Aransas to fish for tarpon as a sitting president. They're big game (so, I suppose, was President
Roosevelt) but you don't have to fish for them from a half-
million-dollar boat thirty miles offshore. I caught one once
standing on the bank of the Colorado River with no camera
in the car.

The fish can grow to eight feet and over two hundred

pounds. It is a glistening silver in the water, a bright metallic shimmer. Blunt nose, silver scales, a husky, muscular body. It is a member of the herring family and has a rudimentary air bladder, which allows it to take oxygen from the air. This facility lets the tarpon do its characteristic rolling motion, surfacing for an instant, a glint of silver in the sun, and then smoothly sliding beneath the waves. Like a porpoise, but they're a fish. I wouldn't attack Flipper ever. Honest.

The tarpon were coming back to our coast, for reasons no one really understood. At Pass Cavallo, which is a wide and deep natural pass on the middle coast between Matagorda Island and Matagorda peninsula, we fished for them from a drifting or idling boat, waiting to spot one or a school and casting lures in front of them.

When a tarpon takes a bait, it explodes.

The fish is a jumper, leaping clear from the water to rid itself of the hook, blasting and jumping with unbelievable force. Should a large one land in the boat after a violent jump, the fisherman's best course is to go overboard before getting hurt, a rather nice role reversal.

It was a rotten thing to do.

"In sickness and in health," right? I rationalized by reminding myself that Tammy had shown no interest in me at the hospital, that she had argued only perfunctorily about going to the clinic, that she had been talking about going back to Houston off and on before this anorexia mess started, that we hadn't slept together for months. It was over, I thought, just not signed and stamped and notarized. But I did want her well.

I am not sure any or all of these were valid.

A frightened loneliness popped up inside my skull when I wasn't having steamy fantasies about my doctor guest, who would be passing Wharton right about now, fifty minutes away, no possible way to turn her back, maybe the lights out and not answer the knock?

I could make a list of "good things," sacrifices made, compromises offered to my relationship credit balance. But the hard fact of an invitation to the doctor lady probably put me into an overdrawn state just by thinking about it.

Dr. Stone arrived after dark in a two-seater Mercedes 560SL, one of the cars I've lusted after for years. This ended my moral debate. Maybe a draw? I was glad it was dark and the Evanses didn't see the car. She was a heart-stopper in beige canvasy shorts and a top that displayed her midriff, an ensemble only the most physiologically fortunate ladies in their late thirties can wear. She had a midsize duffel and a smile and dumped the former on my bed without comment. Obviously, the woman had a pathological dislike for brassieres. She posed in the center of the room, conscious of my stare, and ran a hand through her minimum hair. People chemistry is amazing.

She drank Smirnoff over ice, thank you.

"Why did it take you so long to call, Beaumont?"

"What's it been, three weeks? A man has to think, plan, fear of rejection, you know?"

"I was ready fifteen minutes after we met. So were you, I think. At least it looked like you were—'ravaging me'—in your mind. Why wait?"

I was damned if she was gonna out matter-of-fact me, so I shrugged and asked her if she wanted to bring the drink into the bedroom. I was a bit turned off by what my mother would have called her forwardness, brash and factual merged. Somehow, I lusted after a little romance and a guilty Tammy picture tried to surface.

"Don't worry," said Dr. Stone, "she knows nothing about this. Nor need she."

"You're the doctor," I said.

* * *

It is very quiet in Point Lookout at 3 A.M. I sat on a straightbacked chair in the kitchen, which was a separate part of the large open living area, and didn't turn on any lights.

Perhaps I lacked the strength to throw the switch.

By the time a man reaches his forties, he is at least conversant with several types of females, their wants and needs and desires. And his own preferences are set, habits formed, desires channeled. He knows where he is, what to expect, what he likes, what is pleasing to his partner or partners, what can be expected, what is *verboten* and what is not.

I wore my jeans and I wanted a shirt, but would not venture back into the bedroom to get it.

I still didn't know her first name.

I hated sex.

I ran through the past four hours like watching a freeway-style nine-car pileup in ultra slow motion, mesmerized by what you see coming and unable to tear your eyes away, not wanting to witness yet fascinated. It was altogether out of the realm of my experience, everything I wanted plus everything she wanted, all stage-managed so adroitly that I rose to incredible levels and remained detached throughout, a veteran actor tearing an audience apart, a high-wire act without the poles or nets.

I don't know.

If she had called me back into the bedroom, I would have gone. Totally out of my experience.

She was magnificent, charming, giving. She was selfish, calculating, greedy. She was everything and nothing and I watched from somewhere in the back of my head.

I decided to lie down on the couch. She liked the finger stubs on my left hand, too. Strange.

She was bending over in a sleek black bikini to peer into the oven when I woke. The smell of bacon and coffee filled the room. She looked thirty, a beautiful serene Bain de Soleil model, thirty at the outside. And she could cook breakfast.

"Come, dear Beaumont, we must keep our strength up to catch the tarpons," she said gaily.

"Tarpon, singular and plural, tarpon," I said grumpily and she brought me some coffee. How did she know how much Sweet n' Low I liked?

The toast was perfect, the eggs just so, the bacon crisp and tasty, and I did the dishes as she covered the bikini with a modest wrap for the sober citizens of Point Lookout, made the bed, and fixed a visor cap over her short hair. Said hair apparently was shampooed and tossed and ready. She looked magnificent and I told her so.

"And you are a bull, a tiger, my friend," she said.

"You say that to all the guys," I replied, and she nodded. I told her she must have read the Female Fishing Partner's Handbook before she came down and she asked me if I had any complaints. I couldn't think of one that made sense. I put her car behind the house to keep the salt spray and Evanses' eyes off it. I think Dr. Stone saw through this, somehow.

Even the blasted tarpon cooperated. In between being fish-crazy out of my gourd, I had a sense of foreboding, that this entire episode was too perfect, that somehow Melissa (I asked her for her name finally and she had laughed a wicked laugh and made me pay to learn it) had arranged the whole thing.

We had seven fish in the air before noon, three of which stayed hooked for a number of jumps and one which she wrestled all the way to the boat, a five footer that used up all his energy with a wild display of aerial acrobatics. She handled the Ambassadeur reel and the heavy popping rod like a pro, letting the fish take line when he wanted and punishing him on the jumps. Hell, it was picture perfect and when the exhausted fish was at the boat I asked if she'd be happy with a scale for a souvenir to spare his life and she said of course.

The wind was light out of the southeast, the often-turbulent waters of Pass Cavallo clear and blue, and we could see the shifting sandbars that made the pass so dangerous in a chop. The damn tarpon were everywhere and we left them hitting.

"That's how we fish them down here," I said. "To hell with Costa Rica." I did not mention the previous three trips without seeing a fish and the trip last summer where they absolutely wouldn't hit anything three of us threw at them. But God, they were exciting-scary, chrome-plated fish as big as a man rising silently under the bow of the boat.

I doused the decks, popped us a couple of cold beers, and let her run the boat, once we had got clear of the tricky parts and the giant sand flat inside the pass. We had about fifteen miles of unusually calm and deserted Matagorda Bay to traverse and I felt good and guilty in equal proportion.

I was horny, which is a testimonial to something, and she slipped off the bikini as we cruised home and seated herself firmly on me, doing something extraordinary with her muscles, laughing at my expressions and bestowing a dozen light kisses, as innocent as a schoolgirl and as wicked as death.

She was the perfect woman and she terrified me quietly.

We managed to miss the sand bars and the crab traps and the shell reefs or maybe the boat knew the way home itself, a Grady-White autopilot built in for Beaumont?

She wanted to stay another night, chatting about the fishing, which had been spectacular and taken for granted, although I knew better. But I had promised Mrs. Evans I'd speak to the high school seniors again, Advertising as a Career, and planned to keep the appointment, clean-shaved and able to concentrate. The kids were so damn eager for information, facts, the lowdown, that I wouldn't miss it, sneer if you must. And you can make a career of advertising, as long as you don't take it too seriously. So I would be there and talk about TV and how you start and what to say and go to college for god's sake but keep your eyes open for the rest of the stuff that's out there. I took one last regretful black bikini glance and begged off.

I think this confused her a little, maybe my first points on the scoreboard, and I wanted to explain about Career Day but wouldn't risk the laugh. So she shrugged and threw her stuff together in a flash, thanked me politely and headed down the outside stairs without a glance.

I waved good-bye and wanted to go to bed for twelve hours.

The Evanses' pickup was gone, which meant they had already gone to town and that meant I had all the luck of the wicked. They would probably hear about my sexy visitor but they had not *seen* her, which in country ethics meant they wouldn't ask. I could get away with a denial or a semiaccurate evasion. Not too tasty in the mouth, either one.

I sat on the porch with Bullit. Somehow and some way I should get my life straightened out, learn to be a little less curious, maybe slow down the craving for tension I seemed to need. Maybe I'd do that next week. But it had been a helluva twenty hours, that much was certain.

"Advertising is not all glamour, guy," I said to my dog, "but it has its moments."

6

W HAT DO YOU MEAN 'gone'?" I
shouted.

The pretty secretary was flustered and tried to control it
with overly precise diction. "As I have explained, Mr.
Beaumont, your . . . friend . . . has been transferred."

"And who in the screamin' fuck said that was okay?"

"She *is* an adult and she signed the consent form. You're
holding it in your hand."

"But she wouldn't, she couldn't, she wouldn't leave
without telling me."

"Mr. Beaumont," she said sympathetically, "she did."

Tammy's parents were divorced and I vaguely remembered a tale of bad blood between all hands and nobody
exchanged Christmas cards, much less presents, anymore.
Maybe that was one reason she was receptive to an older

guy. But she was definitely on her own, not a comeback child in the extended family of the Sunday supplements, and transferring away was a Tammy-like gesture. I couldn't believe it nonetheless and went barging out in search of Dr. Stone. Damn it, I paid for the insurance, if nothing else.

Dr. Stone couldn't be disturbed. Another Thursday group.

I banged into her inner office anyway, feeling that I had some rights not normally associated with advertising agents and counselors, and caught the good doctor watching a porn movie. Group grope, bad lighting, and the actors weren't all that pretty. Must be an old one.

"Getting tips?" I asked before she switched off the set.

"Mr. Beaumont, you are interrupting me in my work!"

"Tough job." I nodded to the now-blank TV. "I'm your tiger, remember?"

Her lip curled and I had the distinct feeling that any further tarpon fishing or Stone-exploring was receding fast. I couldn't decide if that was good or bad.

"Who said Tammy should be switched out of here? A sister facility. And where is it? And how in the fuck—"

"Be quiet," she said sharply. "You have no legal or ethical say in this matter. It is entirely between Tammy and her doctor."

"Hitler Number Two? That's probably where this whole pro—"

"There is no problem."

I looked at her and tried to superimpose the wanton woman of my bay-house bed on this rigid figure. She had moved to stand in front of me, in my "space," and she was taut with anger. Her voice remained controlled but my testicles drew up protectively.

"Doctors are not god," I reminded her.

"Nor do we wish to be. We do, however, have a better idea, a less emotional idea, of what is most beneficial for the patients."

"Just tell me where she is."

"I will not. I cannot discuss a patient with someone who is not even a relative."

"Oh, come *on*! This is Beaumont."

"And here I am Dr. Stone and what I said stands."

I walked in a small circle. For a minute I had the mad thought that Dr. Stone had arranged all this just to have her way with my body. A second glance at her disabused me of that notion.

"Look," I said. "I'm obviously concerned and I obviously care about Tammy—"

"I am aware of your concerns," she said flatly.

"All I want to know is where she is."

"To what purpose, Mr. Beaumont? If Tammy had wished you to be aware, to visit, I am sure she would have made arrangements—"

"She's nuts! I mean, shit, she's in a mental hospital."

"She is in a psychiatric facility for an eating disorder. I concur in the diagnosis. This does not mean she is incompetent in any legal or moral sense."

"Jesus Christ!"

"He too would probably be confined here should He choose to return." Now she softened, the joke was obviously a mood-breaker, and took my arm. "Sit down and calm down. You don't want to be a patient yourself and I'm afraid none of the M.D.s on the staff are capable of dealing with a stroke anymore. We're all out of practice. Would you like a cigarette?"

"Well, shit, Melissa, I feel responsible. No."

"None of us are ultimately responsible for anyone but ourselves. Children an obvious exception. Don't worry about Tammy, Dr. Natelson is extremely good at what he does."

"Still, there's no reason why—"

"Hush," she said, shaking my shoulder lightly. "Hush and show me your . . . designs? . . . for the new brochure.

I'll check on her for you, but show me this first. Go on. I promise to check."

It wasn't as if Tammy had been kidnapped. With a plus-$25,000 capabilities brochure as the bait, I allowed myself to be sidetracked after more reassurance. We pulled out the layouts. My artist lady had done a fine job, die cut, blind-embossed, varnish on the color subjects and all. We attacked the fears and questions of people confronted with the need for a psychiatric facility head-on and in simple English, which was a breakthrough in itself. It's hard for civilians to conceptualize a brochure from the layouts we do, thumbnails and roughs, so I had the artist make a stock dummy, a mockup of the brochure on the paper and to size. Then I had her do a thumbnail, small-scale indication of every page in order. Finally the typewritten copy, and I went over the whole mess with Dr. Stone.

Who apparently could visualize. She made a few changes, winced at the price quoted, suggested a change in one of the proposed photographs, and approved the whole shebang, enriching my next month's billing considerably.

"I still want to know where Tammy is," I stated as I packed up the layouts and stuff.

"I'll talk to Dr. Natelson, get progress reports," she soothed. "Will you take me to play pool tonight?"

"Pool? Will you wear a low-cut blouse?"

"Need you ask . . . tiger?"

"Oh, Jesus, Melissa, that's so corny."

"But effective, is it not?"

I didn't know she was a pool shark. Probably had a custom-made, two-piece cue, in a fitted leather case, black velvet on the inside. Eight-ball Melissa. Dead-Eye Melissa.

Hell yes, it was effective. I've seen the movies too.

Tammy should have told me. Trying to tell me something. I wonder who put the idea in her spiky head?

A LARGE ACCOUNT CAN consume a small ad agency. Since most of my attention and efforts were focused on the clinic and all the odds and ends they discovered I could do for them, I had found myself spending the better part of every week in Houston.

The shrinks were much like any other client, only a touch more aware of their rarefied status as healers. Mostly, they were aware of their symbiotic relationships with the insurance companies that footed the bills. A metaphoric clearing of the throat and straightened posture when discussing methods and means of public communication, pompous language and what did the other guys do, no mistakes in public, please.

Seemed like the current thing to do was to check into the hospital if you had a mental hangnail and I wondered what all the ministers and grandmothers were doing, now that their traditional aid-and-comfort roles had been taken over by the mental health professionals.

I talked brochures (dignified) with M.S.W.s and television spots (too expensive) with C.A.D.A.C.s. Occasionally, I bumped into a real M.D., most of whom I found vague and distracted and not eager to make a decision. The patients wandered around looking rather cheerful, by and large, a far cry from the hellish mental image I once had of such facilities. The overhead must have been a killer, even with 208 beds. Most of which were filled, praise the Lord.

"Putting programs together" was the cry. This entailed discovering a DSM-III category of disease (which included virtually every possible sort of mental disorder and some I doubted existed) that needed fixin' and then whopping up a course of treatment to fix it. One needed to ascertain if the insurance companies would pay and if the program could be sold to a public that seemed eager to lap it up. The therapeutic benefits and the insurance possibilities ran neck and neck sometimes, not always, but enough to set your teeth on edge.

Actually I met a couple of doctors and a therapist or two who seemed more concerned with the patient's welfare and needs than their own aggrandizement. And the quality of care was really first rate, at least to my layman's eye. It was a pleasant place for a mental health facility, blues and grays notwithstanding. Nobody seemed nuts and everybody was all too eager to share and relate and deal with your troubles or their troubles or troubles in general.

God, they talked. Patients and therapists. And talked and talked and talked with no real regard for my time, which was what I had to sell. If I hit them with a bill for said time, they screamed like an outraged eagle, as if the "learning experience" offered me should be pay enough. But their phones kept ringing as we ran the media.

Patients were discharged and we needed to fill their beds

although I did a quiet bit of follow-up on my own, research, and discovered that they did seem better, functional, still with problems, who the hell doesn't have them? But capable of functioning after discharge. That made me feel better and the ads showed it.

We struggled with substance abuse on the radio and warned of the hidden horror of eating disorders (which I could write from the heart), talked up an intensive care unit for the unfortunates who had both mental and physical problems, took time out to offer a program for learning disfranchised kids (the announcer cocked an eye at me and asked for an English translation but I made her say it until she got it right), and the phones just kept ringing.

So did my personal cash register. Personal success makes me queasy, nervous.

I managed a day or so every other week in Victoria and I was living in "Executive Housing" off Richmond and the Southwest Freeway, which was a modified motel room with a kitchenette and some fairly nice dishes and pots and pans supplied.

I did brochures and flyers and small space ads and was working hard on the big brochure, which had now escalated to over $30,000 because we had to add a four-page signature to incorporate some additional treatment modalities and two photographs of therapists left out. Egos were involved.

Dr. Natelson flatly refused to tell me where Tammy had transferred and why. He insinuated it was none of my business and I insinuated he was a commie quack. We did not part company on the best of terms. I knew I wasn't discharging my self-appointed responsibilities well but waffled in the face of so much white-coat authority. Besides there was Melissa, and she promised me that things were going well.

The day that I discovered that Tammy was gone, I also discovered that Melissa didn't own a two-piece pool cue.

She did manage to whip me rather readily, using her blouse to the utmost, to the point that I had to buy dinner. The other players were quite sorry to see us leave. We wound up at her house, naturally.

Her bedroom was as bare and functional as an operating room, a king-size bed low to the floor, some kind of satin or silk sheets, and a comforter that I felt I needed immediately. No pictures, no mess, no female sprawl of cosmetics on the Scandinavian teak dresser. A Sony twenty-five-inch TV was built into the wall along with a VCR. An Eames chair sat in the corner with a marble cube, marble ashtray, and that was it.

The house was in Tanglewood, originally designed as a stepping-stone community for up-and-comers who couldn't quite afford River Oaks, where the oil barons played. Now it had a prestige of its own. Her place was in the more expensive section, on a large lot. Lot, hell, three-quarters of an acre, and I suspect she didn't mow the lawn on Saturdays. Perhaps ol' Horce came out and gnawed it down with his brown teeth. Two stories, red brick and ivy, colonial pillars out front and a day servant couple who kept everything compulsively neat. Most of the rest of the home was Houston-opulent, a lot of dark wood cabinets and chairs with knobs. Big rosewood dining table and chandelier. Two sunporches. Copper implements hanging in the kitchen. I wondered about her income because the place had to be a mortgage handful, even on a hotshot doctor's pay.

She was, if possible, even more avid and demanding and aggressive on her home turf, as blunt and matter-of-fact as the male of myth, although I learned long ago I shouldn't be that way.

I did note rather ruefully that Tammy guilt seemed to be diminishing and told myself that it was reasonable since Tammy had chosen to make herself unavailable. Or maybe that too was a rationalization. Once inside the clinic, though, she had shown no sign of interest in me, as if this was a way to break up gracefully. I suppose there are worse. Should I worry more? Hang around with shrinks and you question everything. Except the bedroom. Especially the bedroom.

I did hard duty in that bedroom.

In point of fact, Dr. Stone and I became an item quickly, quite detached and professional at the hospital, but a teen-age fantasy at home. Not that we spent all the time in the bed: she seemed to have an inexhaustible interest in all sorts of things. We ran Malibu Grand Prix racers on the little track out by the Southwest Freeway and attended opening night at the Alley Theater and we found a funny little soon-to-be-gone French restaurant that had few pa-trons but excellent food. Melissa ordered for me in what I suppose was excellent French. I got even by looking up my elderly Spanish waiter friends at Houston's oldest Mexican restaurant and asking for *"las tostas y queso, por favor."* The waiter asked if I wanted salt with my chips.

I managed rather adroitly to avoid any further pool-shooting, Burnt Beaumont Dreads Flame.

She had a boy's fascination for porno flicks and we had a permanent MasterCard deposit at a nasty video store. She was a critic of the orgasm, ridiculing those who were faking it, pointing out sexual deficiencies in plot, structure, and acting and applauding those few that met her criteria. I re-mained only mildly aroused, although her excitement al-ways proved contagious in the end. And she would smile secretly.

"Worn out?" she would tease, and I always said no.

We stayed away from the Foxy Lady although she did insist I take her to some of Vince's competitors. I avoided Vince's place and I didn't take her home to Mother, either.

When I would protest that perhaps we were seeing too much of each other, she said, "No commitments, no strings." And became unavailable for days. When I managed to reestablish contact she would whisper lurid details of her escapades. I never knew whether they were real or some porno imaginings, to the point where I would attack her and attempt manfully to re-create the deeds her words portrayed. The secret smile appeared again.

My personal Puritan ethic was taking a beating as was my sense of male-female roles, a healthy awakening I thought but one that made me inherently uneasy, a generation of subconscious typecasting being torn apart. She told me she could not and would not interfere with Dr. Natelson's judgment on the question of Tammy and suggested that I would be doing the patient no favors by persisting in inquiries. Before we could get fully into discussion, she would do something physical and totally distracting.

"This way, this way," she would mutter, face tight and lips set, quite sure of her needs.

And she was equally good at defining and discerning mine, the shrink at work perhaps, but giving, zenlike, in order to get. Sometimes I would pull back, stubborn, resentful of her stage management, dominant male genes bursting in my psyche. And I would catch her watching me, a metaphoric nod, and feel uneasy.

At rest period, I would suggest that perhaps she was a victim of her own training and experience, a weird sort of unhealthy osmosis drifting depraved thoughts from her patients' brains into hers, and she would snort and accuse me of being provincial. "Few of us fully exploit the sensual," she said once, and I wondered if we had enough time.

When she felt she had me nailed up good and tight, she showed me her secret treasure and in the showing broke whatever sickish bond had grown between us.

She was a doctor, for god's sake.

8

I HAD TO CONFESS to somebody and I gave Vince the black bean. He had called once, which was a rarity, and left a message on my Victoria answering machine. So I showed up at the not-so-smoky Foxy Lady, picked a table by myself, and sipped a bourbon.

Somebody male had been coaching the girls because a duet was on the stage, street clothes, what a sound idea, slowly undressing each other to the pounding music with much simulation of lesbian frenzy. The ordinary blouse and skirt and slips and bras made it semireal and very sensual.

It moved my well-sated sexuality and I speculated as to the cause, deciding finally that middle-age folks like myself had been indoctrinated so hard in the myth of female disinterest that this crude portrayal of raw same-sex desire hit us where we lived. I applauded like a bastard.

Melissa was at a meeting in Dallas. I wished she was sitting with me because she had mentioned exotic sex, a third-party male or female joining us, more than once. I couldn't handle that, another male especially, some insecurity that she laughed at and suggested she'd have a girlfriend join us, "Not just for you, Beaumont, though I expect you'll find it fascinating?"

"You're not jealous a bit, are you?" I had said. She was right about the fascination, of course.

"I am sure of my own sexuality. And aware of deficiencies in others. One had best take what one wants, for no one will give it to you," she had replied shortly.

I stopped and mentally shook myself. "Jesus, Beaumont," I said in my head, "you're acting like a horny teenager and that's not real appropriate for a person your age. What the hell is happening?" And a sliver of fear passed over me.

A large hand reached over my shoulder, grabbed my glass and sniffed, and Vince snorted. "I told you not to drink the bar shit," he said. "Come on back."

I followed him to his private office, not able to resist peeking into the girls' dressing room, a large area populated by not-clad or half-clad ladies who returned my gawks with colossal indifference. Three of them had to see the boss right then, but he waved them off and closed the door to his office.

Fresh drinks fixed, he silently saluted me with his glass and raised an eyebrow. "So?"

"So . . . what? Business is booming, the stuff is working like crazy, most of my stuff in Victoria is under control, and I haven't been fishing in three weeks. Boy, did we nail the tarpon awhile back."

"And?"

"And I'm getting back into the same old shit I used to be in 'fore I got chased out."

"Actually chased yourself out, didn't you?"

"Whatever."

"And how's Tammy doing?"

"Oh, fine."

He looked at me. And looked at me.

"Fine, really, Vince. She's doing fine."

He looked at me.

"Okay, I don't really know. I haven't seen her in three weeks." I glugged some drink. "The doctor seems to think it's best, that she doesn't need any outside pressure now, you know." More drink. More stare.

"Jesus, Vince! Gimme a break!"

"This is the lady-doctor with the tits?"

"No, Dr. Natelson. Nerd type with a moustache."

"What's with the lady-doctor?"

"She's not Tammy's doctor, that's the other guy. She runs the hospital, her specialty is relationships." And I blushed.

The phone rang and Vince chewed on the guy who apparently had been sending him some steaks that didn't meet standards. He chewed in the quietest tones possible, with horrific threats somehow behind his mild words. The guy apparently decided to come right then with replacement meat.

"What you and Tammy do is not my business," he said to his glass after he hung up. He looked at me. "But I won't have her hurt. You're chasing the doctor now, right?"

"It's actually the other way around, I think. Yeah, we're . . . involved. You know, Tammy and I, before this anorexia stuff, we were—"

"Not my business. But you're a good guy and she's a neat girl. You need to be actin' that way. I can't speak for her but I would think she'd like some support along about now."

"Hell, I would, I'd like to. I just don't know . . ."

"What?"

"I don't know where she is," I said miserably.

"She's in that clinic. Down toward Galveston, right?"

"She transferred."

"Where to?"

"I don't know." He waited. I shrugged and got up to fix another drink. "She transferred and doesn't want me to know which hospital she transferred to."

"She tell you that?"

"The doctor did. You know how they are, Vince. This is so because I say it is so, doctor-as-god."

"So Tammy didn't say 'go away.' The doctor says that she wants it this way. And she's got no parents, right?"

"You really know how to hurt a guy, Vince. Tammy has parents but . . . they're not close."

"Point is, the shrink-lady's telling you that Tammy has abandoned you. The shrink-lady also has hustled you, you're telling me."

"The other doc, Natelson, says the same thing."

"He works for her, right?"

"What are you trying to say? Spit it out. Jesus, I never got to what I wanted to talk about."

"You'd better go find out where Tammy is and how she's doing. I want to know and you *should* want to know. Doctors ain't god, no matter what they tell you."

I remembered saying something similar not so long ago. I nodded and he changed the subject, but it hung over our conversation and I decided to make an early night of it.

"Don't forget," he said as I left. I nodded and shook his hand, feeling guilty and angry that he had to remind me of my obligations. I had spent a long time getting rid of the garbage that most folks called their obligations, but this one was real and Vince was right.

"Hey, Vince," I said in parting, "you ought to change your name. Take out the 'n.'"

He didn't think it was funny either. On the way out, the same two girls were at it again, their turn had apparently come up in the rotation, but it was less wonderful. Much less wonderful. I was sick of sex, girls, and Beaumont. Mostly Beaumont.

I didn't confess to Vince after all. Didn't get around to telling him that Melissa had taken me into her confidence the night before, as a grand finale before her Dallas trip, and I was sickened and frightened and aroused all at once. Some stuff was too strong for me, some invasions of privacy too much for even a snoop like any good adperson.

We were lying in bed, she in bikini pants only, one of my fetishes discovered early on, the contrast between the clothed man and the enticing female pleasant and mildly erotic for us both, and she proposed we watch a movie.

"You want me to go get one? What's your pleasure? Group stuff, two girls? Maybe a nice orgy?"

"No, darling Beaumont, I have some special tapes for you tonight. Something few people have seen."

I had looked at her quizzically, because in our few weeks of dirty movie repertoire, I think we had seen virtually every sort of configuration. Maybe just bits and pieces of the best ones. She went into her study, I watched the strong motion of her thighs and hips, and came back after a minute with an unmarked tape. The study stayed locked.

The tape blinked to life on the big Sony, no titles, only some obscure numbers and a man and a woman were undressing on the screen. The porno flicks had only a few actors and actresses and I had come to recognize most of them, but these people were new. And not spectacularly attractive. The woman had long black hair, sixties hippie style, carefully tended, which I liked.

Their undressing was a touch awkward and they made nervous jokes, the sound quality rotten as usual, and they began to kiss and make love. There was something different about the tape, a documentary quality, and I couldn't see what it was until I realized the camera position never changed.

The timing was different also. In the movies, generally the girls began feigning preorgasmic arousal in about a nanosecond while this couple kept at what they were doing for longer periods of time.

"These aren't actors," I said.

"No." Her face was close to mine and she stared into my eyes, hers enormous, although it was difficult to take my eyes away from the screen. The voyeurism quotient was right up there.

These were not especially beautiful or well-endowed people and they made no attempt to play to the camera. When the girl's hair fell forward to obscure the action, she let it fall. The groans and moans seemed real, the exclamations natural, and I was in somebody's bedroom and not at all sure I was comfortable with it. Advanced relationship group, she had said. Did they refuse comment until they could see the films on Monday afternoon? Or was the camera Melissa's little nontherapeutic secret?

"Do I want to know where you got the tape?"

"Perhaps. Does it excite you, Beaumont?" Her hands found the answer quickly and she began to stroke me slowly, gauging my excitement with touch and with her huge eyes on my face.

"You didn't really . . ." I was having trouble forming thoughts and expressing them. On the screen, the man had pinned his lover's hands above her head and she twisted against them, obviously enjoying the temporary bondage. Their pleasure in each other was nice to watch, even though it wasn't nice to be watching. Would I care if it was me?

"What? What didn't I do? What wouldn't I do? Watch." And she bent to her task with harsh enthusiasm, holding me just below the level of release, and I couldn't take my eyes off the damn screen. I was a voyeur, a window peep, and my heart hammered in my chest, breath half caught and clogged in my throat, and I watched two people make love in front of a camera, transgressing and excited by it, she wouldn't let me alone or give release, she wouldn't, she couldn't, and I yanked her up and began to duplicate the action of the screen, her eyes staring holes through mine all the while until it all went black and overflowed.

"I have more for you when you wish," she whispered sometime later. "Interested?"

I was decidedly postcoital. She packed for Dallas while I dozed and I left late at night to drive to my motel home, scared and more than a little sad. Probably what I had thought of as porno movies when I barged into Melissa's office before were more of the same. They had to be patients and the sex had to be therapy and I hoped it worked. I doubt whether the patients knew they were also performers and the whole thing made me slightly ill.

The undeniable fact that it was also arousing didn't help my nausea. I didn't like myself. I liked the idea of Dr. Stone using this stuff for personal pleasure even less.

I could have jumped up and left. Coulda, woulda, shoulda.

I would cheerfully window peep, should some pretty person leave her shades up and I stumbled upon it, that seemed like the luck of the draw. Or perhaps a secret thrill for the peep-ee, a harmless power trip, okay? But videotaping patients in your care, people who had trusted you with their most intimate thoughts and feelings, seemed like a horse of another hue.

And I had watched. Not too fond of ol' Beaumont right now.

9

Dr. Stone's secretary was an exuberant redhead, much given to semi-sexy remarks, and not abashed to make jokes, mild jokes, with me about my relationship to her boss. I was a familiar figure in the hospital by then inasmuch as I had been virtually everywhere, tracking down docs to get approvals, interviewing therapists, sitting in as an observer to get the feel of group sessions and CARE therapy and this and that.

CARE therapy is not a bondage game but a mild outdoor obstacle course, taken as a group, in which the individual learns to trust the other members of his or her group in the matters of knots in ropes and will they catch me when I jump? It's remarkably effective, on a basic physical level. The group sessions could be quite dull or explosive, and it was interesting to watch the therapist play peer pressure to bend the wills of stubborn patients.

I had been through all this stuff and I was a wanderer and a poker of my nose in all sorts of places, excused on the grounds of research. So Sherri, the secretary, wasn't surprised to see me early the next morning.

"Here on business, I presume, since Dr. Stone is out of town," she started.

"Now that she's away, it's you and me, kid."

"Be still my heart. Whatdaya want, Beaumont, it's time for me to go get coffee."

"Take off. I just want to leave a note on Mel—on Dr. Stone's computer."

"You know how to work it?"

"I get along. Did you turn it on and boot the disk this morning?"

"Every morning. I don't usually let people in her office, but since it's you . . ."

"Start planning for the weekend, okay?" I waved her away and went into Melissa's office. The computer was what I wanted.

I wasn't afraid of the infernal machines, but I did have a respectful mistrust of them, like you do feeding a large and half-trained dog. For years, I had pounded out my copy on an aging manual Smith-Corona with dirty keys. Then I graduated to a Selectric and, once I mastered the idea that the backspace key erased, loved the clean copy I could produce. I held out against word processing on a PC until the end but when I converted, I believed my writing improved measurably, if only because it was so easy to edit and hone and revise.

My agency had a rudimentary bookkeeping system setup on an IBM-AT and I could stumble around in RAM and ROM until I got what I wanted, even if I did get there by a circuitous route.

Plus Melissa and I had played with the computer in her office a bit, so I approached the keyboard with confidence.

Misplaced confidence. I faked up a funny letter and stored it there as my cover story and then tried to access some of her files. I needed a password and nothing I tried seemed to work. I tried "Dr. Stone" and "Melissa" and "1/10/53," which was her birthdate. I tried her phone number and address. I tried the license plate number of the Mercedes and "560SL." "Incorrect" beeped the machine.

I tried "fuck" and "sex" and "psyche." Nothing. Then I yelled for Sherri and bluntly asked her how to get into the mainframe.

"Why do you want to do that? That's where Dr. Stone keeps all her patient records."

"That's why I want in there. I'm doing a series of case histories. You know, 'This Is Sherri. We Cured Her of Her Sexual Addiction' kind of stuff."

"You didn't," she said, but leaned over my shoulder and keyed a string of numbers and the screen blinked and showed me a directory.

"You're sure Dr. Stone said this was okay?" she asked nervously. "It's real confidential."

"I am your full-service agency, remember? Besides which, I just want to make a few notes, I'm not going to print out anything, but Melissa wants authentic ads."

She edged away, back to her desk, still muttering about confidentiality, but I waved her off with a great show of confidence. The deliberate "Melissa" might have helped.

Patients were listed by their diagnosis, by their doctor, and by their insurance company. I found Tammy quite easily as a Natelson patient and glumly read the admission diagnosis, the proposed course of treatment, and the insurance claims. Follow-up notes were sketchy. The file ended with "Transferred, B Unit," and a date two weeks earlier. What was B Unit?

A directory file did not list a B Unit and there didn't seem to be any A Units. I called up file after file and found nothing. Then I went back to Natelson's patients and looked for others who had been transferred to B Unit. I found half a dozen, maybe 10 percent of his caseload, and scanned the biographical data on a couple. Nothing emerged. Sherlock Holmes was needed. Several other doctors' patients had gone to B Unit too, but I couldn't make a correlation.

I went back to the directory so Sherri wouldn't know what I was digging into and went out to her desk. "What's a B Unit?" I said with my most charming smile.

"I don't know anything about a B Unit," she said sharply. "And I really believe you need to stop poking around in there. I'll call Dr. Stone if you need more, but I can't—"

"Hey. I'm through. But one guy seems perfect for an ad but I need to interview him and the file says 'B Unit.' So I need to know where—"

"I really wouldn't know. Now I'm going to shut down the computer. I shouldn't have let you—"

"Hey, your secret's safe with me. Melissa wants good ads and the ads are as good as the information, right?"

"Well, let her tell you about . . ."

"About B Unit?"

"I don't know any B Unit!" And she whipped into Dr. Stone's office in a rush. I could hear her tapping the exit instructions on the machine and called good-bye.

I could just imagine the report Melissa would receive.

But it was worth it if I could locate Tammy without going through legal fuss and major threats and world-class problems, not the least of which would be the loss of my shiny new client. I'd do all that if I had to, but the sneaky seemed better.

I wasn't going to face Vince without firsthand information about her. Hell, I wasn't going to face myself.

10

As it happened, it was simple. I merely swiped their morning mail. I had, as a matter of practice and inclination, made friends with the two switchboard operators (so I could independently monitor telephone response to my radio commercials for one thing) and all secretaries. I had observed that their mail went out in two shifts, gray mailbags and the whole bit, and they took it to the postal substation in Clear Lake City.

So on my way out, I bought myself a cup of coffee in the cafeteria until it was time for mail and managed to show up at the front desk when Betty the receptionist/operator was gathering it for the morning post-office run.

"Hey, I'll take that for you and save you a trip," I said. "I've got to buy some stamps this morning."

"Would you mind?"

"I'm going to the post office anyway. Bring your mail sack back tomorrow."

She said thanks and it was too hot to go out if you didn't have to and gave me the sack. Which I lugged to the Blazer, put in the seat beside me, and drove away, feeling like James Bond Number Two.

And when I found a convenient Circle K drive-in, I stopped and got myself a cold Corona and parked off to the side and did a sort. The air conditioning in the Blazer kept things comfortable and I sorted through an impressive stack of mail until I had isolated three letters, addressed to individuals without initials behind their names, all in Freeport, Texas. All to the same address. Personal mail, forwarded, I suspected. I knew all the chain's hospital locations in Texas and the surrounding states because of my ambitions to syndicate some of the marketing, and Freeport was not one of them.

It was an hour's drive, I had an enormous load of guilt to dispel, and most of the rest of my life was under control. So I copied the address and took the mailbag to the post office as promised. I bought stamps too, no liar Beaumont.

Highway 35, which runs parallel to the coast and Freeport, was an old friend. I used to drive it after work in my faithful VW bug when a damp-eared copywriter, trying to use the long summer days to get in a few casts at the tarpon at the mouth of the New Brazos River. They had widened and straightened the road and now the drive was a breeze. The car may have had something to do with it, too, my old VW wouldn't completely stop, but it was known to falter now and again.

I think a geologic time glacier formed the Texas coast, melting to make the Gulf of Mexico. Something had scraped the land flat all along the coast, brown prairieland furrowed by what had to be stubborn farmers and studded with mesquite trees and pumpjacks, which were roughly equal in durability. I remembered an old rancher telling me

how he cleared his land by suspending a logging chain between two big yellow Caterpillar D-9 tractors and driving
them forward to uproot the tough mesquite. "Then"—he
had snorted—"the blasted things grew back inside a year. I
burned 'em, plowed 'em, dug 'em out, and they still came
back."

Mesquite charcoal was now all the rage and if the trend
caught on, perhaps greed could conquer our indigenous
tough tree. Maybe all of Texas was like that: we had been
caught in a full-scale depression that nobody mentioned
when the oil prices went belly-up and were in the process
of bouncing back, bigger and better and hopefully wiser.

Freeport's a funny small city. The beaches are perhaps
nicer than those at Galveston, forty miles to the northeast,
but the town has been long dominated by a couple of giant
chemical plants. Big tax base means big clout and up to a
few years ago the plants polluted like crazy and nobody
said "Boo!" I can't prove this scientifically, but I had been
at the edge of the Gulf, the ocean, and seen the sickly
yellow-green water come rolling down the river and you
could smell it.

Under the burning sun, the town looked twice-baked. If
you turned left off of 288 at the bedroom community of
Clute (home of the Mosquito Festival) you went to Surfside
Beach and the teenage maidens and their raw and loud
consorts. Bikinis and beer and the "Jesus Is Lord" surf
shop. A big marina and an impressively high humpback
bridge over the Intercoastal Waterway and its barge and
commercial traffic. If you continued onward into town, you
passed the giant chemical plant and a bunch of major highway rattyness, pizza shops and tackle stores and rundown
cars and abandoned two-story "office" buildings plus a
beer joint or two, which I wouldn't enter without body ar-
mor. A brave motel or two, big high school plant (Texans,
even poor Texans, put an amazing amount of their tax rev-

enues into school facilities, which gives teenage riots and drug dealing a central focus but keeps it off the streets, right?) and a monument to the shrimping industry, which needed it. Three weeks on a rusty fifty-foot boat in the Gulf is no picnic, far removed from the relative luxury of the offshore oil platforms.

I got a map and some overpriced gas at a Shell station and headed to the western fringe of town and the road to West Columbia.

The road cut through a lush cedar and mesquite and live oak forest that looked like something from the Amazon River basin, and there was no address like the one I had copied.

I U-turned and tried again, we're talking a mile or two of nothing where the address should be, and found a small oyster-shell road leading off the highway, obscured coming the other direction by a big live oak. So I bounced on down the narrow roads, trees and brush crowding both sides, figuring that I could ask directions if nothing else.

You could see what had happened in a glance. Somebody's dream went bad and the results lay baking in the Texas midsummer sun. It had been a ten-unit motel, the signs and stuff were gone, but ten little cinderblock cabins remained, arranged in a U shape, with two cinderblock structures put together for the office. I can see the owner-couple planning, making projections at the kitchen table. "Honey, all we need is sixty percent occupancy and then we'll . . ."

And when the tourists don't come, all the people who had been so eager to help are crowding each other, jostling to shove their demanding palms in your face, pay me first, no, me. And each day goes by and you sink in a little deeper, an ear cocked for the car turning off the highway, sitting in the office watching a secondhand TV flicker and listening for a car, *please* a car. I shuddered.

As I sat there conjuring up images—hell, they might

have made a bundle and retired to Maine and left the motel
here, what did I know?—a small unpleasant guy emerged
from the office unit. Unpleasant because he was carrying a
shotgun. Jeans, one of those shiny-sleazy short-sleeve
shirts they sell at Wal-Mart, and a white straw cowboy hat
with feather. I never can figure what the feather means. Or
what bird suffers for their glory, when it comes to that.

I got out of the Blazer slowly, trying to look friendly,
both hands in sight and moving carefully. "Looking for
12990," I called with a smile.

"Found it," he said flatly. The gun was dangling from his
right hand like he had forgotten it, a pumpgun of some
sort, barrel showing some signs of use, blueing a little thin.
He did seem like he was familiar with it.

"This was supposed to be B Unit?" I said, trying.

"Is."

"Well, good. I'm here to see one of the patients, a
Tammy—"

"Nope."

"Wait a minute, all I want to do is say 'Hello,' see how
she's doing, just a quick visit, you know?"

"Nope. No visitors."

"Dr. Stone said—"

"Dr. Stone didn't tell me nothing. No visitors." He didn't
emphasize his refusal with the gun because he didn't have
to.

"Hey, friend, what's the harm? I'd like to see her just for
a minute. I've come a long—"

"Ain't gettin' any shorter."

We stared at each other. It was a scene out of *Deliverance*
and I knew what happened in that movie. One of the window A/C units cycled off with a sigh and a wheeze. I could
feel the perspiration popping out on my forehead, rather
more forehead there to sweat these days. My best smiles
and friendly body language weren't working. I took a cou-

ple of steps toward the nearest cabin and the gun started up and I stopped.

"You call this Southern hospitality?"

"I call it private property."

I could see or sense movement from the cabins, eyes at the corner of the windows, whispers perhaps floating to my subconscious, a bit of color visible.

"Suppose I come back with a cop?"

"Suppose you come back with the sherf. He'll tell you this is private too."

Two sentences. That seemed to be the extent of his dialogue. The shotgun remained pointed in my general direction. I shrugged, saluted, and got back into my car. He didn't move until he was out of sight in the mirrors.

I checked into the cleanest motel I could find when I was back in town. Seemed like I was spending a great deal of time in motels and pseudomotels these days, and I wondered if my burgeoning bank balance justified it.

I planned a bit of quiet trespass. I also wondered if the insurance company was paying the going rate, full medical and psychiatric service, clean hospital environment, for ten cabins baking in the brush. I wondered if Tammy was eating, was she happy, treatment working, insights into her relationship with an aging ad biggie.

A seedy liquor store had Old Crow and ice and I poured a bit of courage into myself and wondered where I dare have dinner. I missed Bullit, strangely enough. She was probably pining for me too, at the Evanses', unless it was dinnertime.

11

It GETS DARK AT 9:06 Daylight Savings time in summer in Texas. This is an Old Crow approximation. I had poured rather more courage than needed, and several cups of coffee at the restaurant that served me fairly good fried shrimp had made me a wide-awake drunk at best.

So I was exceptionally slow and careful as I retraced my drive out to B Unit. It lacks the glamour of Iwo Jima or even Pork Chop Hill or Da Nang.

I parked well down the road, grabbed the black metal five-cell flashlight from the console, adjusted my newly purchased long-sleeve navy-blue pullover, and was off.

The woods are considerably spooky at night even when you *know* that the last tiger left Texas long ago. I remembered vaguely that there had been quite a stink about a rancher who was purchasing worn-out zoo lions and organizing hunts for them on an island in Matagorda Bay or somewhere. I hoped he hadn't mislaid any lions.

I also wondered about dogs. Shorty and his hat looked like a dog owner. Not a friendly soft animal like Bullit, but something in the Doberman line, lean and black and full of hostility toward intruders.

"I hope they're red Dobermans," I whispered to myself. "That way I can see 'em to whomp 'em." And took a couple of practice swings with the flashlight.

Daniel Boone I was not. I bumped and stumbled and ran into things and finally ended up walking down the drive. No moon to help, maybe it'd be up later.

I slowed up considerably when I could see the lights from the cabins through the bush. I did a rather masterful sneak around to the back window of the office only to discover my friend of the afternoon watching TV. Tiptoeing away, I headed for the first of what had been the rental units.

Which had the blinds down, of course.

With both ears pointing back toward the office and listening hard for the scrabble of claws on the drive, I eased up to the window and peered through the gap between the miniblinds and the sill. Two fat ladies were watching TV. Neither was Tammy and/or anorexic. Cabin number two had the lights out but I peeked anyway and I think one bed was occupied.

Cabin number three had more TV watchers. I began to yearn for a conversation, even a fight. It was summer reruns, for god's sake. A crossword puzzle. Scrabble?

Cabin number four had Tammy and another girl.

She looked better, although I somehow doubted that she was getting very intense therapy out here. Everything in all the cabins looked transient, no pictures on the wall, no mementos on the dressers, like the motels they once were. If my theories were right, my dear friend Dr. Stone and crew were working a scam on the insurance companies and the patients were the ones to suffer for it. But she did look better, a little meat on her bones.

Probably because she'd been away from me for a month.

The TV was on here as well and the other girl, a non-descript blonde, was closer to my window than Tammy. What the hell, don't sign on if you can't take a joke. I walked around to the front, keeping my navy-covered back to the lights from the office, and tapped on the door.

I had my finger to my lips when the other girl opened the door but she still screamed softly and I winced.

"Jesus, don't you know what this means?" I whispered, tapping my finger vigorously against my lips.

"Wha, who are you?" She was skinny and her nipples were up under a T-shirt.

"I'm Beaumont and I need to talk to Tammy. Quietly. I don't want the dogs to hear me."

"There aren't any dogs here." She stared at me in amazement.

"Well, shit. The guy with the gun, then. Can I please talk to Tammy?" I tried to look harmless.

"You're cute," she said.

I didn't have a snappy rejoinder for that. "Tammy!" I said. "Please."

"Well," said the girl, "I'm really more attractive than she is. And I haven't had any for five weeks and three days and seven hours and—"

I pushed past her and Tammy emerged from the john at the same time, the other girl almost clinging to my arm.

"Beaumont!" Tammy said.

"What's wrong with this woman?" I asked.

"She has a sexual disorder," Tammy said.

"I have a sexual disorder," the girl said simultaneously.

"I'm sorry," I said. "Are you ready to boogie out of here?"

"No," said Tammy.

"Sure," said the girl.

"Jesus," I said, sinking to the couch. "I don't believe this."

"I don't believe you're here," Tammy said. "Or why."

"I'm here to rescue you, get you back to the hospital, get you straightened out, and I'm in imminent danger of being blasted by a load of buckshot or chewed on by the Dobermans," I said miserably. "If I wanted to do snappy lines, I'd of found a bar."

"I don't need rescuin'," Tammy said. "I'm feeling better, although I think we need to have a serious conversation. What Dobermans?"

"Sure," I said. "When?"

The other girl was rubbing my shoulder with a rather possessive air and explained, "He must have a deep-seated fear of Dobermans."

"With Dr. Natelson present," Tammy said primly.

I shrugged off the other lady and she said, "You shit!" and started to scream at the top of her lungs.

"Fuck!" I said. "You sure you're okay?" Tammy nodded and the other girl took a deeper breath and I was gone. Behind me I could hear Shorty shouting something but he didn't shoot. I was a mess when I got to the Blazer, running through the woods does that, got the door open and started and burned rubber away from that crazy place.

We had a motel room meeting: Conscience, Practicality, Ethics, Old Crow, and me. As in many meetings, the results were inconclusive. I could hardly complain to the police since Tammy seemed perfectly content and had refused to escape. I, technically, was in violation of the trespass laws and they probably could get me for window-peeping to boot.

I didn't want to wrestle Short Stuff for the shotgun either.

I wasn't some Avenging Knight of the Good, going around righting wrongs and rescuing maidens, especially maidens who didn't want rescuing. But I had signed on for treatment for Tammy and treatment for Tammy was what I planned to get.

Even if I had to lever it out of sex-crazed Dr. Stone, who may well have been a smashing therapist, but who was too weird for my taste.

I think.

12

WHEN I GOT BACK TO Houston, full
of high purpose and residual bourbon fumes, there was a
message awaiting me on my Houston answering machine.
All the comforts of home in my Executive Housing suite
now, the manager herownself had moved me into a larger
unit when I turned out to have the longest tenure of any of
her customers. And it was better, like an apartment where
they did the sheets once a week. I always wanted to somehow connect my Houston answering machine with my Victoria answering machine and see if together they couldn't
conquer the world.

My blueline and chromalins were ready.

What this meant is that I was ready to get approvals and
move into the payoff stage of Dr. Stone's brochure. The
blueline proof is the last, failsafe check before you actually

commit to printing a brochure, and the chromalins give you an idea what the color is going to look like. We fussed over color work on the press (sometimes to the point of angering the pressman) but if your separations weren't right, you'd never get a pleasing final result and the chromalins showed you that.

My hungover brain, perhaps beating up on Beaumont out of guilt, changed my normal priorities and resolved to settle the Tammy issue before getting the proofs approved. It was getting to the point that I did not wish to be involved, which seemed to be the thrust of Tammy's position, and I wondered how you could drift so far apart. Hell, we were waterskiing in opposite directions. But I wanted them to do right by Tammy. I called for an appointment and found Sherri to be cold and correct. She confirmed that Dr. Stone could see me at two. Perversely, I told her that was not convenient for me and how about four?

She checked and that was okay and I went to the "Y" looking for an unsuspecting young 'un who would be hanging around the racquetball courts seeking an old person to humiliate. I surprised more than my share of flat-bellies this way.

Two hours later, maybe three pounds lighter, showered and feeling the surge of energy you always experience after violent exercise, I drove toward Clear Lake and the hospital. My brain cells were fully oxygenated and I felt super. A last-minute victory in the tiebreaker, a matter of cunning and court sense over sheer energy and youthful reflexes, didn't hurt a bit.

Sherri acted like I was an insurance adjuster or bill collector when I arrived and Melissa made me wait fifteen minutes. I lounged a lot, put my feet on the furniture, and annoyed the redhead with a steady line of patter, which she grimly ignored.

When I was finally admitted to the inner sanctum, my lover was not pleased. It was a bit nervous-making but I could fake it. I didn't need body language or subtleties to figure out her displeasure, she shook her head and said, "In my experience some persons have a syndrome of causing difficulties for themselves. I fear you are beginning to fit this pattern, Mr. Beaumont."

"So formal," I said. "Aren't you the lady who was shouting something about 'breaking in half' not too long ago?"

"It is ignorant to confuse these two things," she said quietly, and I knew she was right. I sat down, stretched out, still enjoying the supple looseness my old muscles had obtained on the racquetball court.

"How are things at B Unit?" I asked.

"I suppose that is intended to intimidate me?"

"You pick. Intimidate, square away, straighten out, whatever. I want Tammy out of there and back where she's supposed to be."

"You presume a great deal."

"I presume you don't want your third-party payers to know the degree and extent of treatment facilities you offer at good ol' B Unit. They might be a bit testy about this."

"Perhaps. Or it could be a useful adjunct to therapy."

"Oh, gimme a break."

"No, think about it. How do you know and why do you presume that our 'third-party payers' do not know about B Unit and C Unit? And fully approve of the treatment modalities in force at both? Are you qualified to make these judgments? And, moreover, how dare you come in here to threaten me, rather unsubtly? Just who do you suppose you are!" The last phrase was not terribly cutting for a sophisticated lady shrink and she stubbed out her Winston angrily. Then lighted another. How could she keep her mouth tasting so good?

"Calm down, Dr. Stone," I said. "As you once told me, the M.D.s here are not a good choice for stroke."

"Very well," she said, with a too-visible effort at control.

"Suppose we forget this entire matter and get on to work. I assume the package you brought is for me?"

"Proofs on the brochure. But let's not change the subject quite so quickly. I want Tammy out of there and back here where she belongs. She looked better—"

"You've *seen* her?" That was a no-no. Of the two small dangling members of my body, my tongue causes the most frequent difficulties. Melissa was visibly upset, body assuming an attack posture. I had apparently gone from an annoyance to a threat.

I decided to blunder forward, all throttles locked in Full Ahead. Damn, I should learn not to show my hand before the last bet. "I drove to Freeport yesterday."

"That is a closed facility. Patients are there precisely because they need no interaction with nonpatients. You have breached a serious—"

"Oh, bullshit," I said. "Patients are there because it probably costs you a dollar and a half a day to keep them there. And you get, what did you tell me?—five thousand a week? Five thousand times ten motel rooms that you picked up for a song times two people to a room. Means a gross of a hundred thousand a week on B Unit alone, right? I really don't care about the . . . scam, shall we call it? But I want Tammy treated."

There comes a time in a poker game when you're running a bluff and you realize you're bluffing a wired hand, you can't win. And your heart sinks a bit and you have to decide, no expression change on the face, please, whether to press on or bail out. Bailing out is recommended. Something like this happened during my speech, but a smart-ass, show you! urge pushed me on and I told her all that shit. Complete with prices, way to go, dummy. Near as I could remember, I didn't owe the insurance companies anything and maybe it was just another treatment facility, who was I, et cetera.

Her hands clawed a bit, face reddened. For all of that,

she was controlled and quiet when she finally spoke. "In this state the laws are quite precise, Mr. Beaumont. Quite. Any citizen can swear out an affidavit in probate court alleging that another citizen appears to be irrational and out of control. A threat of bodily harm is taken as evidence that the second party is, in fact, out of control and is sworn to in the affidavit. The probate court then issues a warrant for the second party's arrest. This is arranged through the involuntary detention of the person by the constable's office until a full and complete psychiatric examination can be held."

She looked straight at me and there was an emptiness in her eyes that made me think of the old western adage that the Indians used to turn the captives over to the squaws for torture. The lady Indians apparently were better at it.

"Naturally," she said, "it is considered unseemly for the person who swears out the original affidavit to hold the psychiatric examination. I, for example, on those sad occasions when this has become necessary, have always used one of my colleagues. Dr. Natelson is most cooperative."

My laugh was hollow. "Then we get out the rack and thumbscrews, right?" Surely she was kidding.

"We have much more sophisticated methods available, should the patient need restraint." She wasn't kidding. I began to wonder about edging to the door. They couldn't put you in the loony bin that easily. It was your word against theirs . . . theirs had some heavy initials behind the names. But even so, she should know, and I suddenly was frightened.

"Let us not talk about such matters any further," she said suddenly. She'd decided something. "Show me your proofs and let us move on. I assure you Tammy is in good hands. What have you got for me?"

I liked this even less. We played stare-across-the-desk. She won, I suppose, since I slid the proofs from my briefcase and came around to her side of the desk. We had skipped the denouement somehow.

It was too easy. We flipped through twenty pages plus covers in about two minutes and I couldn't get her to really read the text or study the clever way we had incorporated rules, lines, into the design to lead the eye through the words. The color chromalins zipped across her desk equally fast.

Actually, her hurried perusal was probably much like that of a real reader, I reflected glumly. The ad business was in some ways like preparing a scrumptious meal for people who gobbled. Everything was wonderful and her compliments had a distracted quality as if she were focused elsewhere.

"Okay," I said. "We've got about two weeks on this, not rushing the printer, and I'll check the color on the press. Which will be at three A.M., it always is. We're looking at something on the outside of thirty-two thousand dollars total, plus tax. It's because of the extra pages and color subjects."

"It will be quite nice, I'm sure," she said. "I like it, Beaumont, you do good work." She wasn't grudging about it, as clients often are, afraid that even faint praise will jack up the price. And the stuff was good. The earlier threats, if they were threats, receded.

I put the stuff away, glanced at the door to make sure it was closed, and went over behind her chair. I started to rub and massage her shoulders and she leaned back against my hands and closed her eyes. Gently I said, "Hey. We don't have to fight about this other stuff. Just bring her back."

Eyes closed, she muttered, "You will not give up, will you, darling?"

"Nope." Still rubbing. I wanted to slide my hands down over her breasts but restrained, in the office.

"I will . . . consider what you say. Oh, that feels good." I rubbed the knots in her muscles for a bit. She said offhandedly, "Would you also stop by the Group Room on your way out? There's a new Sexual Antagonism group starting and I wonder if we might make a promotion out of it." She twisted to look back and up at me. "Maybe it will turn you on."

"Didn't know I needed it. I'm not kidding about Tammy. Okay? Sexual Antagonism? Are we for it or against it?"

"Please, enough. Now go." And she gave me a playful push and was lifting the phone before I cleared the door.

At the door, I said, "You are going to do something about Tammy, right?" She waved an impatient hand at me, so I shrugged, took it as assent, and left.

The Group Room was a bare, carpeted, windowless conference room kind of place, carefully swept clear of potential weapons. Most of the furnishings were bolted to the floor and walls, so an enraged group-person (groupie?) couldn't use them as a weapon. It might have been a sensible precaution, since I had seen tempers and tears and rage and jealousy and the whole spectrum of emotions yanked out of people by group pressure.

I must have been early, the room was empty.

The first two members of the group were male and rather large and wore white T-shirts and white pants and soft-soled shoes. I knew that couldn't be right.

When they moved in on me with small smiles and reassuring words, I was convinced of it. When they grabbed for my arms, I exploded.

13

At least I didn't waste any breath in futile protesting.

That was as much as I could say for my performance against the white-clad thugs/attendants. I am a fairly large person and in reasonable shape for a guy who drinks too much and worries a lot. My racquetball performance had surprised more than one younger person, one that very day.

But you get so far removed from the physical. The pushing and shoving matches that we called fights were back in high school. As an adult I avoided situations where the winner was the guy who was still standing. I was not prepared mentally to use what strength and agility I had to hurt somebody else.

Not even when that somebody was shoving me down a

hospital corridor to a fate I had zero interest in and a room I didn't want. I must have known what was happening when they came for me, because I came out of the chair fast, feinted toward one, and tried to run over the second.

While it didn't work, I had a momentary flash of pride that I had responded quickly enough to fake them out for a second. I bounced off Thug A and sent him reeling back against the wall with his back across a chair, which must have hurt. By that time, the other one had an iron grip on my arm and shoulder and was attempting to rack it up behind me. He was twisting my wrist in toward my back and that let me pivot around to half face him, in position to clobber him with my left.

But I hesitated, some vestige of civilization or fear making me pause, and that gave the other one time to come in from the side, avoiding my backward kick.

I did manage to make a muffled fuss, cracked up some furniture, hurt one of them with a flailing elbow, but before you know it I was under control and out of there. In the corridor, I could lunge enough to move the two of them from one wall to the next and our progress was a series of lurches and jumps and drags, breath coming harshly and loud, grunts, muffled exclamations, and moans.

I won't say my opponents were discussing baseball scores or talking about girls while they wrestled me down the hall, but they seemed generally unperturbed and that made me even madder, if possible. I grimly remembered Vince's offhand remark about streetfighting, "Hurt the other guy first and fast, eyes or balls are best, but first is most important." And I wished fleetingly for my old friend, tougher than I surely, more realistic, an answer for problems like this, which didn't come up in my ordered existence. For a mad moment, I thought the whole thing was a classic case of mistaken identity, not me . . . you want that other guy, no offense taken, fellows, but get it right in the future, okay?

They acted like this was routine. Down the hall, into a room, a room in one of the locked wards I realized, and simply held me there, surging back and forth as I struggled and lunged. Nobody said anything. In some strange way, this seemed appropriate and I didn't tell them they were making a mistake, that I would write my congressman or have their jobs for this.

When the nurse came in with the hypodermic, I went berserk.

Up to now, I knew that something was big wrong and that I had opened my mouth too much and that I was being taught a lesson and that Dr. Stone and company were as shady as I feared. Or worse. But the nurse and the needle brought it all home—these fuckers were going to drug me, take away what self-control I had, control me— and I panicked. Now even the two attendants paid attention to my struggles and we bounced around the room for quite a while, from bolted-down bed to the several walls, knees, elbows, nails, teeth, they were *not* going to stick whatever strange stuff into *me*, red killing rage. No, not into me, nurse shrunk back against the door, waiting for an opening, and I ended up on my face, clothes ripped and aware of some bleeding, one of the attendants swearing softly, a hard knee crushing against my shoulders, feet flailing uselessly, immense suffocating weight on my back, twisting my arm more than necessary, they wanted to hurt and the prick of the needle in my butt, no worry about sterile procedures here and in what seemed like a moment I was floating.

Like most semi-curious Americans of my age and inclinations, I have had some experience with drugs. I knew that marijuana didn't automatically qualify one for a life of abject misery and degradation à la *Reefer Madness*. Cocaine (and I gave thanks for this, knowing my addictive personality) had about the same effect on me as a good cup of coffee and I was happy for it. Who needs felony convictions and a hundred twenty bucks per brown vial for a mild lift? Even when the price went down, I could pass on snort with no regrets. I had never been sure enough of my psyche to be interested in exploring it with the aid of LSD, blotter acid or whatever form was popular. Heroin was for junkies. My first wife's doctor used to prescribe amphetamines by the hundred for weight control and all they did was make me nervous. So bourbon was my drug of choice and less and less of it as I grew older and less able to withstand it.

This was brand-new and would have been terrifying except that suddenly I lacked the capacity to worry. Whatever she shot me with separated me into three distinct and unrelated components.

I was conscious of my reality position, who I was and what I was and what the dispute was about. This in the same remote and uncaring way that I knew the starving children of India would really appreciate the food I didn't want to eat when a child. I wanted Tammy back and the doctor to knock off the scam, I knew this and I was not pleased that she had used this method of having her way. *But I didn't care.*

I was conscious of my body, the feel of my clothes, the position of my hair, the way my limbs were arranged, the fact that they were undressing me and all of this felt rather nice, sensual in a disembodied way.

I was conscious that these people, even though we were in dispute, were really being rather nice to me, caring for me, arranging me on the bed and covering me with the sheet and blanket and didn't the blanket feel nice? As I concentrated on the way it felt, I could feel myself becoming erect and I was pleased with this, wanted my friends to see it and know it showed how much I appreciated all the nice things they were doing. I *liked* it. Weren't they proud of me?

These thoughts shifted slowly and pleasantly through me, one then another, and I thought perhaps time was passing because the faces that appeared over the bed seemed to change now and again, but it was nicer to concentrate on the way the blanket felt and how I could shift from one place to another and create a whole new spectrum of feelings as long as I did it slowly and when would those nice people come ba k?

I was especially pleased when Dr. Stone appeared above my face, smiling at me, she liked me, of that I was sure, and memories shifted slowly in my mind. She smiled at me, see I told you! and said something and I forced my mind to focus on her.

I remembered that she was doing something I didn't like, travel, motels? But we had made up because here she was, coming in and out of vision as she fussed around the bed, she must have cared. I smiled at her. She talked funny, brushing at my hair, nice Dr. Stone. Melissa.

"A form of synthesized neuroleptic, which interferes with the transmission of neurological impulses at synapse points. It does make you feel good, doesn't it, darling?"

I smiled at her to show her I understood and felt brilliant for doing so. I knew she'd like that and it was important that she see how much I wished to please her. She was a doctor, after all. She leaned down and wiped my mouth and I smiled again.

And again and again.

14

I COULD GAUGE THE passage of time
by the reactions of my conscious-but-uncaring mind. When
they used the Demerol, I was more agitated but less capable
of movement, this must have been during the day. At
night, they used the original injection (given now with
nursey efficiency, cotton swab with alcohol, careful injection, bare recognition of a pinprick in my rear) and I could
move better physically but only wanted to confine myself
to small sensual movements in the sheets.

At times I idly wondered who would miss me. This had
to be a short-term solution, because I had bills to pay and
clients to service and who would check the proofs at the
printer? Somebody had to look at the color when it came
off the press. Did anybody care? I didn't.

Everything was in the abstract. Some self-preserving

memory made me resolve to struggle, to get up, to flee, and there was a sense of panic at the end of a period, before the nurse came in to give me another shot. I was bathed, shaved, fed, and medicated, and they praised me when I used the bathroom successfully. Everything was very pleasant.

One of the nurses was a gray-haired lady, plain and stout, and she muttered to herself as she prepared my injection or brought my food. Something always was bothering her and I tried to smile at her to make her feel better, like me. She'd wipe my mouth abstractly and I could hear fragments of sentences: "I can't believe . . ." "This is not right, she's overmedicating . . ." "There's something wrong with this . . ."

Once she had words with Dr. Stone, on what I think was the third visit, and I was quite disturbed in a languid way because I wanted everything to please the doctor. She was my doctor, after all. But the older nurse had apparently said something or asked something and Dr. Stone was shouting and the nurse hastened to give me my injection.

Bits and pieces of anxiety floated around and I'd try to grasp them when I was alone and didn't have to concentrate on pleasing the nurses. I knew something was wrong. But I didn't care because everything was so pleasant.

On what I think was the third night, Dr. Stone came in with a man, a man I knew and didn't like but I figured I should try to please him too, so I smiled. He had a small moustache and I knew from somewhere way back he was a doctor too. Like Dr. Stone. They were talking by the foot of the bed and I kept raising my head to see and couldn't control it and would fall back on the pillow. Which seemed rather amusing to me so I did it a couple of times for the pleasure of it.

From then on, they stopped the shots and we played a game called Pill. Open wide, let me see it on your tongue, got it? Good. Now swallow for me, there's a good boy.

And, anxious to please, I'd swallow. The new way was nicer really, because they didn't have to stick me, although the sticking wasn't really bad. Nothing was really bad.

And if it hadn't been for a bad piece of meat, I might still be there playing Pill.

My main meal was served in what I thought was the evening and I always looked forward to it, although they could have let me use the knife and fork like I used to. I had a clear memory of using knives and forks. But they fed me and talked and if I did good and ate everything they'd be happy so I always did. The food was mushy, mostly, I couldn't taste anything all that well.

The younger nurse fed me, some grayish slightly smelly meat, but I chewed and ate and she gave me the pill and left. Now I could think, or try to think, to bring together the fragments of memory that disturbed me, all night long. I tried to think but it was impossible.

Suddenly I was quietly sick to my stomach, not a violent upheaval but sick, and I got most of it off the side of the bed and got through and lay back and wondered what I should do. I had never been sick before and I was afraid of the nurses, extra work for them, perhaps I should. It smelled bad. So I scrunched over to the side of the bed and waited. Perhaps I could tell them it was an accident.

In a couple of hours, I was nearly rational and in a cold rage.

15

T<small>HE PILL MUST HAVE</small> come up with the rest of my dinner and it was the evening meal so I'd had better than ten unmedicated hours. I wouldn't say I was back to Beaumont-normal, but some of the haze lifted and I understood what the bitch had done to me.

What I didn't know was how long she had been doing it, what day it was, what had happened on the outside, and whether she had had me legally committed to the hospital, as she had so carefully explained.

For damn sure, I was leaving.

I lay there soiled in the locked hospital room, trying to control a panic that threatened to paralyze me, knowing that I wouldn't get another chance to rid myself of their drugs.

Unless, of course, I could remember to vomit on cue,

never a favorite pastime. The residual effects of the drugs made my mind skitter and bounce but the lethargy, the uncaring idiocy, was rapidly leaving. What I needed was a watch and mine had gone with all my other pocket litter. I had a sense that several hours had passed but I wasn't sure how close we were to morning and the morning pill.

My mind had the frenetic quality you reach in a certain stage of drunkenness, bouncing rapidly from thought to thought, even breathing in short pants. I arranged the pillows under the covers on the bed, amazed at how physically clumsy I was, as if the "body" in the bed was half out of it. Then I crouched by the door, knees creaking, and listened.

The door opened inward with the hinges on the outside, a necessary precaution in a locked ward. The bed and bath were both to the right side of the room as you entered. I huddled on the left.

My time sense was screwed up. When my legs began to cramp, I'd get up and try some rudimentary exercises, conscious of how silly I looked in the hospital gown, listening hard. Then I'd resume my crouch.

My coordination was coming back and I did push-ups, enjoying the strain on my muscles. Listening all the while.

When she finally came, after I had dozed a little and almost died of heart failure when I realized I had fallen asleep, it was the nice, middle-age nurse and that almost proved my undoing.

She opened the door and, as I had hoped, hurried over to the dummy in the bed. I was right behind her, fist raised, ready to swing but couldn't. Instead I grabbed her from behind, hand over her mouth, and said urgently, "Don't move, keep quiet!"

"Oh, my god," she said muffled.

"I'm sorry but this whole thing is . . . a frame-up and I'm not supposed to be here, I know all the patients would tell you that but Dr. Stone and I, I mean she's got me, oh hell, give me that damn pill."

She made noises and clenched her hand around the little paper cup with the pill but I got it away from her and tossed the nasty thing on the bureau. She tried to get loose and I tightened my grip, hurting her.

"Jesus, I apologize," I said inanely.

We stood in an insane tableau and I was in terror of somebody coming in the door, so I forced her down on the bed, ashamed of the awkward rape similarities, and held her there. I didn't know any wonderful judo holds that would put her out and I didn't want to hit her. I wished it had been Melissa, I wouldn't have felt compunctions. I could smell a sour smell from being sick and it made me ashamed. She indicated she wanted to talk to me and I eased my grip on her mouth and she said, eyes wild, "Don't hurt me, I'll be quiet."

"That's okay. But if you try to make noise, I'll have to."

"Who's your doctor?" Odd conversation. What's your sign, do you like horses, come here often?

"I don't *have* a doctor," I said. "This is a frame-up. I found out something—B Unit—and Melissa, Dr. Stone, had to keep me quiet somehow so she stuck me in here with your happy juice."

"Not mine," she whispered. "I thought they were over-medicating, we just have that compound for clinical trials."

"It works, you'll see."

"You won't . . . do anything?"

I couldn't figure out what she was worried about for a minute and suddenly realized she was afraid of rape and I started to tell her that I couldn't be less interested and stopped. "No. Not my style, though I'm tempted of course."

Her eyes were becoming just the slightest bit unfocused and I kept watching the door and reassuring her she was safe from me, a major struggle with my libido, but safe. "I'll have to tie you," I whispered, and she nodded vaguely and I got up, poised to spring back at her, and covered her up. I started to get rid of her lace-up nurse shoes but decided that would be a bad move. I made a modest effort at tying her, using the covers and sheets, careful to be as non-threatening as possible. The pillowcase made a fine gag and I tried to apologize. Finally, I figured she was effectively immobilized. I tie good knots.

I moved away to listen at the door and came back to check her but she showed no inclination to do anything but lie there.

I kept trying to make a list in my head—pants and shoes and money and my keys and a way out of the locked ward—and losing track of where I was on the list and starting over. I still had no real sense of how much time had passed and was seriously thinking of trying to fit into her nurse uniform when the door swung open again and it was my old friend Dr. Natelson. "Miss Agreemont! We *do* have other patients you—"

He made a most satisfactory moan when he hit the floor and I put him in bed after I grabbed his pants and shirt and white doctor coat plus keys and money. My fist hurt and I enjoyed it. Found the pill intended for me and gave it to him. Take your medicine, there's a good boy. Had to stroke his throat like a dog to make him swallow, yuck. I struggled into his clothes, wished I had a double dose of that stuff to shove down his throat, and was ready to hit the road. If I could find a clipboard and not have to answer any medical questions I was what you call home free.

Dr. Natelson, predictably, drove a Mercedes. His pants were too tight and too short. I had walked briskly down the corridor, heart thumping away like a horror movie and fighting a recurring vertigo, timed my arrival at the entry door, also locked, so I arrived when somebody else was coming in with their key. I nodded a good morning as they held the door for the doctor and got the hell out of there. Never had anything felt quite so fine as leaving by the doctors' entrance off the side of the hospital. The doctors' parking lot was conveniently located right there and I simply started at one end of the Mercedes and Jags and Lincoln town cars until Natelson's key fit. One commie drove a Chevy and I figured it was an intern. Natelson's car was a black 300SL, littered and dusty.

I also figured I had best put some miles between me and the hospital and headed for Houston. The nurse and Natelson would be undiscovered for something between ten and twenty minutes, I suspected, plus another ten minutes of general milling around and fussing and then this car and ol' Beaumont needed to be out of sight. That gave me enough time to get to the area around the gigantic Almeda Mall, just about ten miles south of Houston. Acres of parking, 102 convenient stores, and the normal complement of car thieves, I hoped. My driving was not the best and I had a tendency to unfocus, but I kept the big car within the lines and below sixty-five and that's what counted. I got to the shopping mall without a single siren or red lights flashing in the mirror. Parked in an uncrowded row and left the windows down, keys in the ignition, to make it easy for the thieves too.

Teach him to mess with my old brain. But I felt a little bad about leaving the car, predictable or not.

Several people looked at me strangely as I hurried into the mall and I realized I was swearing out loud, fists clenched, not quite a stagger in my walk.

Maybe I needed some psychiatric treatment, no thank you.

I would burn somebody bad for this.

16

In what was the clearest thinking I was capable of, I called a cab, after checking Dr. Natelson's wallet to make sure we had sufficient funds. The sonuva-bitch had over six hundred bucks. Obviously, a neurotic need to control via money. Maybe a security symbol. I was quite happy to use it, figuring this was just the start of my revenge.

The cab took twenty minutes to make the trek out the Gulf Freeway to the mall and I'd had to swear on my first-born to get the dispatcher to send one. In Houston, first you get a car and then worry about a place to live. Cabs lead a lonely and not very lucrative life, relying mostly on visitors and the girls from Vince's place who took home astronomical money on a weekly basis, some of it legit, and never could save enough for an automobile downpayment. I used to worry about this but Vince convinced me it was an attitude thing. "Most of them can't figure out which way to turn the key," he stated, with perhaps more cruelty than absolutely required.

The cab took me to my home away from home where they didn't ask questions as long as you stopped in the office each week to sign another Amex ticket. They gave me a key, accepting my lost-key story indifferently. What'd they care? I was the oldest established permanent floating executive in Executive Housing.

I looked like hammered batshit.

I was positively scrawny, for one thing, hollow cheeks and the whole bit. And their shaving attempts had not been entirely successful. The bags under my eyes had bags and I had trouble focusing in the mirror. A shower and shave helped a bit as did my own clothes. I briefly wished for a puzzling crime scene and the ability to plant Dr. N.'s suit pants and shirt in it but finally tossed them in the corner.

"I'll deal with that later," I said, updating Scarlett.

I was having a bit more emotional swing than I liked. Fear that she had indeed committed me and I was currently a fugitive from the funny farm, fair game for law enforcement officers anywhere. "Boy. You funnin' with me? I'm fixin' to call you in, see if yo have any war-ents out, you hear?" Then anger. Lovely scenarios of degradation, public humiliation, and disfigurement for the poised Dr. Stone and assorted cohorts. I'd leave out the nice old nurse who argued with her. I hoped she was loose. Oh, she had to be loose by now. Much fussing in hospital corridors.

I placed a call to my old friend and shrink-of-choice, Dr. Hector Edfelter. Who was "with a patient" and couldn't be disturbed. I needed him. Possibly to reassure myself that the vast majority of mental health care folks were legit and nice and skillful and well trained and caring.

"It's urgent," I stated flatly.

"I'm sure it is, most of our calls are," she said cheerfully.

"But surely you can understand that the patient *with* Dr. Edfelter thinks her problems are urgent also."

"Bromides I can do without, lady. Tell Dr. E. I'm gonna spill the beans about the Chicago convention unless he calls me soonest." Then I repeated the number with insulting slowness and made her read it back to me. *And* made her repeat the message.

I am far too old to take lip from cheery secretaries.

I also had no specific knowledge of my friend's midwestern escapades but had learned enough of his nature to figure there probably was *something* he was a touch secretive about. Especially where Mrs. Edfelter, a tall honeymelon blonde, was concerned. She was the light of his life and the model for all successful relationships, one he used occasionally in therapy, but Hector was all too human and male.

This did not prevent him from presenting his therapeutic views of the ideal male-female relationship enthusiastically and with considerable force. Honesty, empathy, trust, deferring momentary pleasure for long-term success. Nonetheless, I had my sources and was quite ready to cast the first stone.

And the phone rang within twelve minutes, which proved the effectiveness of implied minor blackmail. "Beaumont, what's so blasted urgent?" he asked. "A touch of impotency? Tammy wearing you out? Maybe a confession that she really needs a younger person? You got a real problem or you just worrying yourself nuts as usual?"

"I wish to report that one of your fellow shrinks has had me in the funny farm, full of some joy juice that you guys better keep under lock and key." Make jokes, Beaumont, better than the opposite.

"Do I sound like the Malpractice Committee of the AMA? What's the real problem? You want to do lunch or can you pop for a session?" I wasn't getting through to him.

"Hey, Hector, I'm serious." Voice cracking.

I could hear him adjusting his mental gears. "Okay," he said. "You have been confined? Really confined?"

"In a psychiatric institution," I said, naming it.

"Admitting doctor?"

"I didn't ask." Silence. "Seriously, Hector, *I* don't know. They didn't tell me. I was forced there against my will."

"But you're out now?"

"No, Dr. Edfelter, I'm using the phone in my room and when I get through some nurses are coming in to party. Of course, I'm out. Fought my way out."

"Beaumont," he said seriously. "Tell me all about it."

Hector was a professional listener. Over the phone, he was deprived of his body language, the subtle adjustment of features and position of hands and encouraging little sounds he used when in a session. But he had a sharp, logical mind, little patience with ramblings or sidebars, and a merciless instinct for getting to the heart of whatever matter was ripping you up.

He did this now, with an occasional hum, small whistle, clicking of tongue, single word to fill in a stumble, and made me organize the entire scenario for him in minutes. I held nothing back, except some tricky bed stuff that I wasn't sure he was ready for yet. Besides Mrs. Edfelter would want to know where he learned it.

"I know of her," he said, referring to Melissa, not his wife, "and she has an excellent reputation. I don't believe I've met her. She had a paper in the *Annals* . . ."

"Dr. Edfelter, I'm really not interested in her CV, okay? The blasted woman is running a scam to end all scams and she stuck me in that place when I found out."

"She used a . . . synthesized neuroleptic, you say. There are a number of varieties . . . you were aware but lacked . . . willpower, you say?"

"I was a veggie."

"Interesting." His voice was filled with professional curiosity. I interrupted.

"These were not clinical trials, Hector. The bitch is a crook. She shot me full of happy juice. She's your colleague, for god's sake!"

"Perhaps there's an explanation. If you were to go back to her, calmly now, and demand—"

"I'm not going anywhere near her! Is she right, can she get me committed as easily as she says?"

There was a curious embarrassment in his voice. "In general, the outline she gave you is accurate. There *are* safeguards, but the law states that any person can swear out an affidavit—physical threats—as she said and the courts then have an obligation to confine the threatening person until a proper psychiatric examination can be obtained. Uh . . . *have* you been feeling okay?"

"The examining physician has a sore jaw right now and I doubt he'd give me a very good rating. Of course I'm feeling okay, goddamn it."

"Your options are her superiors or the police." Hector sounded dubious, and who could blame him? "It's hard to believe that she'd do this."

"Hector, believe." The police still probably had a charge or two, stemming from a previous misadventure, pending against me. And she was her own superior, just ask her.

"How 'bout you ring her up?" I asked.

"And just what would you have me do? Accuse a fellow practitioner of assorted felonies? I'd be nuts to do anything like that. You trying to get me banned in Boston?" He sounded annoyed. I'm sure lots of patients would like to pit shrink against shrink. Maybe a TV show: *Dueling Shrinkers*. I went through the whole thing again, trying to convince my friend/therapist I was indeed rational. "Strange" was as far as he would go. And he got upset when I asked him to pressure ol' Dr. Stone, the needle lady. My buddy, my lover.

Sometimes Hector lost his professional detachment. When we played racquetball, he could be goaded to the point where he'd fling his racquet across the court in a rage, which I enjoyed. Nevertheless, in the curious and closed society that is medicine, his word automatically carried more weight than mine, and I went to work.

Blackmail was never actually mentioned but hung heavy from the telephone line. In the end, he agreed to call for a consult. Which would at least make dear Dr. Stone know that somebody with some clout in her world was interested. I would pursue Plan B as soon as I thought of one.

"How do you feel about all this, Beaumont?" he asked at the end, shifting back into his professional mode.

"Oh, shit. I'm mad and I'm afraid and I'm a bit ashamed and I haven't the faintest idea what to do about Tammy. That was coming to an end before all this started and it made me feel very old and very tired and wondering where it all was gonna wind up."

"That's a fair summation. It's called the human condition," he said, and hung up.

17

THE PHONE RANG AS I sat miserably
there. Hector wanting the last word. Or to tell me he would
have to charge me the full session price. I felt a touch better
for the telling, but I still didn't know what to do. So they
were overcharging for Unit B, so what? But this business
against me was truly Twilight Zone stuff and who'd believe? I was ready to blow any necessary whistles, I guess,
but unsure of how to do it.

"Darling, you are incredible!" Melissa sounded like she
was complimenting me on an especially good performance.
I looked wildly around the room, figuring she'd materialize
out of the telephone or something.

"Beaumont? Are you there?"

"I'm incredible, right. You're going to love the malpractice suit my attorneys are placing. So will your backers."

"That's *precisely* why—"

"So are the newspapers, Dr. Stone. Hell, maybe we can get you on TV at last. For free. Ten o'clock news stories, you know? Sex clinic maven assaults ad biggie, that sort of thing. Strange chemicals, orgasmic rites, what a story!" I evaluated my delivery and decided that I wouldn't scare me if I were Melissa.

"Oh, do hush and listen," she said. "I was going to let you out anyway, but I'm thrilled by the way you made your escape. It's only our second escape."

"I'm glad I could brighten your day."

"Actually, it excites me," she said throatily.

"Sorry, Melissa," I said. "My libido seems to be among the missing. Maybe an extended vacation. I'm focusing on how to describe all that shit you shot me with."

"All of the compounds are well within normal therapeutic limits, of course. It actually should help you have a better realization of the work we do, rather a unique perspective for a . . . copywriter? Is that right?"

"What you did was as wrong as it gets."

She was totally unworried and that was frightening. My word against hers again. Lots of medical mumbo-jumbo on her side.

"I can understand," she said professionally, "why you feel frightened and abused. Perhaps a bit confused. The thing is to talk it out, make sure of whatever action and counteractions we both take, understand where we are. If you'll come back to the—"

"I'm not getting near your snakepit!"

"Well, shall we come to see you then?"

"Who's 'we'? Dr. Frankenstein?"

"I've taken the liberty of consulting one of my backers as you call them, a very well-respected businessman who has been most helpful to the clinic and, incidentally, who is one of your strongest supporters. Don Nelson. Don feels we should be expanding your marketing efforts to other facilities in which he has an interest. More billings, is that what you call it?"

"Melissa. You strong-armed me and shot me full of drugs. Why on earth do you think I'd talk to you about anything?"

"Because you're an escaped mental patient for one thing. Because you certainly could be described as 'dangerous'—ask Dr. Natelson. Because there is a simple way out of all this, good for us both. Because, in the final analysis and despite all your pretensions of wild creativity, you are a reasonable person. As well as quite creative."

Did she have me? A part of me wanted to run as far and as fast as I could. Melissa sounded like her actions were routine and normal and perhaps they could be made to seem that way. She still had Tammy in B Unit, dear B Unit of fame. And what would I lose talking to her? Maybe I could take an Uzi.

"So what is your suggestion?" I said.

"I feel sure Don will let us use his office, downtown. Let's meet and resolve this problem. I have patients and you have ads and we both have many more nights to explore."

"You're fucking crazy," I said. "Okay, I'll meet you." *She* was crazy?

She told me when and where and I agreed, feeling like a dummy. I could get a nap and make a purchase. At least my head would be straight and her "businessman" would understand why you can't let doctors go merrily around drugging people they disagree with. And she was right. My word against theirs.

I was still a bit uneasy about that "escaped mental patient" business. I had no desire to prove I was sane.

I'd agreed to meet her, hadn't I?

18

ALL MY LIFE I'VE dealt with businesses and businesspeople. I've been in board rooms and workrooms and labs and isolation chambers. I've ridden up high-rises under construction in the crane elevator and talked to hardhats and CEOs to get different views of the same company. I've been on offshore oil rigs and stomped through cornfields in Iowa at the Farm Show. I've pretended to be a retail salesperson to "get the feel of the product" and I've focus-group interviewed people who used the product and didn't like it. I've watched the ladies on the food packaging line in Louisiana drop one piece of salt pork in the pinto bean cans just before the machine put the tops on and I've watched other ladies lay up fiberglass boats. I've attended annual meetings and given presentations to the Rotary *and* the Lions. I've talked to a CEO on a deadline through the door of his private john and thought of Lyndon Johnson. I've interviewed another in a private jet.

What I mean to say is that I understand businesses, how they think, what they do, what one can expect. Having a meeting is normal and comfortable when you have a dispute, although I wished I still had an office, so I'd control the turf. But I had an edge in my coat pocket and this was business.

That's why I sat in the twelfth-floor office and waited for dear Dr. Stone. In addition, I had resolved the problem I had been having over *proving* what they had done to me with a nifty little Sanyo tape recorder, one-hour cassette, three and three-quarter ips, sitting in the pocket of my sports coat. The Highlands store had a nice selection and I had tested the built-in mike by turning on the TV in my apartment and moving around the cramped space. I could pick up normal conversation easily and I'd feel a lot better when I had Dr. Stone's funny voice on tape, explaining what she had done to me.

Give the AMA Grievance Committee some meat to chew.

I needed to show her too. Needed to prove I wasn't whipped, I could play their silly games, man of steel, shrugs off drugs. "Just say no, Dr. Stone," I muttered.

What could they do to me on my home turf, which was their home office? I expected lies, evasions, a glossing over, alteration of paperwork and perhaps blanket denials. I also expected to be able to handle all of the above. Me and Sanyo. So I waited for them. Eagerly, even.

The sweet young thing adorning the front desk was not sure how to treat me and had solved the problem by talking on the phone incessantly after she discovered I wanted no coffee. In a few minutes she waved me into the inner office.

"Beaumont!" Melissa greeted me. "How clever of you to

get free and then be wise enough to come here. Isn't he clever, Don?"

Don was almost ready for a cover story in *Texas Business*, if that publication is ever revived. Five-ten or eleven, the black obligatory three-piece suit, just a touch shiny, funny Italian elf shoes, clean desk, minimum personal stuff in the office, a set of golf clubs in the corner for god's sake, various diplomas and certificates discreetly on the wall. Helluva handshake though and I was reminded of Horce. Melissa looked wonderful, colorful and sleek, like a copperhead. I casually stuck my hand in my pocket and started Sanyo.

Don didn't waste time. "He has offered some rather serious charges, Dr. Stone. Five million dollars' worth of insurance fraud was mentioned." I felt smug for a second.

"Oh, no!" she said, grinning. "It's quite a bit more than that."

He looked serious for a beat and then laughed. "Only eight cents a share," he admonished.

"But that turns our earnings from mediocre to quite good?" she said seriously. "And it will exceed fifteen million, from the alphabet units this year, I believe."

"And that gets us both a rather generous bonus," he chimed in. Oh, they were a happy couple.

"I think we earn it, don't you?"

"I think we're about to," he said, looking at me.

"I knew I shouldn't have settled for a would-be Fortune Five Hundreder," I said. "Nothing personal." I was getting mad. "Don't you know what this bitch has you involved with?" I asked him.

"Before you do anything . . . precipitous? let us discuss your alternatives and options," said Melissa. "You're very dear to me and I wouldn't want . . . anything hasty?" I decided her weird speech habits were phony.

"Melissa, you're incorrigible," Nelson said fondly. Another scalp for her belt, I presumed. What could I do? I put my feet on his desk.

"Let's," I said.

First, they assured me that they were not doing anything actually illegal. They were providing care for the patients. In point of fact, some patients actually preferred what they called the "alphabet units," which reminded me of alphabet soup. Perhaps the expense associated with the alphabet units was less but was that not merely good management technique? I was getting good stuff on tape and let them talk, identifying them by name and title when I spoke.

"Overhead down and profits up. Makes sense," said Nelson.

"The unstructured atmosphere can sometimes be a therapeutic aid," said Melissa. "I may do a paper on it."

"But the psychiatrists are still getting a hundred fifty a day for patients they never see and the charge is for a hospital room and all the assorted paraphernalia," I pointed out. "Not a grungy motel, ex-motel room, at six or seven hundred a day."

"Survival therapy is quite expensive and the patients live in tents. If they're lucky," Melissa remarked.

"If you were so confident that this didn't need hiding, I wouldn't have been forced into the hospital," I said.

That was a mistake, Melissa admitted. But I had frightened her with what she rightly perceived as my determination and she needed time to deal with it. Incidentally, she said, Tammy was doing well and had gained more than five pounds, due to therapy.

"How can she get therapy in the boonies!"

"Sometimes that's just the therapy she needs," she said primly, and I thought of Point Lookout, which was about as boonies as you can get. "The zinc helps," Melissa added.

Stepping neatly around the basic question, they offered me an additional clinic to promote, the return of Tammy to the Galveston Bay facility, and a quiet cancellation of the commitment order that Melissa had, in fact, put into effect.

"So now any hick cop can throw me in the slammer as a fugitive," I said bitterly.

"Only if we report the escape and we haven't done that," Melissa told me.

"Yet," Nelson added cheerfully.

"Everybody cheats a little on insurance." Melissa winked. "But you do not wish for Dr. Natelson as your primary mental health care provider. In the near future?"

"Yeah. Fifteen mil a year and going up," I said. "What do your other investors think about all this?" Our conversation was so typically business it was hard to remember we were talking about an insurance scam at best and some form of kidnapping or something at worst. It sounded normal even to me, the victim.

"We haven't burdened them with the details," Nelson said. "Very busy and effective people who trust us to do our jobs profitably and give us the authority needed."

"She's really getting better?" I asked. "Tammy?"

"Dr. Natelson is quite pleased. Not with you," Melissa reported. "But Tammy, I believe, is on the road back."

"And you'll get her back to the real hospital."

"Of course, darling. I never should have allowed her to go to B Unit even though she fit the profile perfectly."

"Lemme guess. An insurance company that's not too nosy, no close relatives around to pester you, and a non-dangerous illness." I figured I had enough and started to stir, ready to leave, enjoyed the meeting.

"You were around, but I thought I could keep you distracted," she said flatly.

"Toss in a third hospital, with the same or bigger budget, and you got a deal," I said, lying through my teeth. I liked what I had on tape, but they had sounded so reasonable, I wondered about persuading the DA. Or whoever you complained to about illegal experiments with mind-altering chemicals. At least, I was in a better position now. "Think about it," I urged.

They looked at me skeptically. Don baby made a note.

"But how can we trust you, darling?" Melissa asked. I looked at her unhappily. Damn, it's hard to lie to shrinks successfully. They hear so much of it. Nevertheless, it was a good question.

Nelson adjusted his face.

"Perhaps we could 'capture' the patient and continue his evaluation," he said sincerely.

"Shit, no!" I said, getting up. It would have been cooler if I sprang catlike to my feet, but I miscalculated and my loafers hit the floor with a crash.

"No violence in the office," he said hastily.

"Well, you can forget that shit. There's gotta be another way, but no way am I going to let you get your needles near me."

"Remember, sweet Beaumont, I'm your doctor," Melissa said. "It even says so in the court records of Chambers County."

"Doctor knows best." Nelson smiled. I didn't want to jump precisely into the center of the frying pan, having just vacated the fire, so I started to edge backward.

Something stung the back of my neck and I spun around to confront a happy Horce. I had forgotten Horce, maybe repressed his ugly ass. Melissa had given herself plenty of time to fetch him—unannounced—to the meeting. He had a strange apparatus in his hand. I started to step up and take that gadget from him only to find my legs weren't working.

That seemed amusing.

Melissa came around the desk and patted my cheek. Then she felt around and found my tape recorder, raised an eyebrow at Nelson, and tossed it to him. "Naughty," she said.

This couldn't be happening in an *office*. Nelson was unrolling the tape from the cassette, I saw blearily. Looked like fun.

19

Everything seemed rather amusing. I smiled faintly to myself in a vastly superior way. It seemed of little consequence that I was lying on a table in a small, unfurnished conference room on the fourth floor and that my shoes and belt had been removed along with pocket litter, money clip, and credit cards. I still knew I was superior. They would come to this realization soonest. I had lost the capability of independent movement or I would have walked out and explained it to them. I had been there an hour or two feeling superior.

Melissa walked in with a hypodermic. Probably thought that she could have some sort of effect on me with another one of her playtoys. Hardly likely.

Somewhere inside I was vomiting and having heavy diarrhea but it wasn't getting to the forebrain. A distant itch.

"It's a derivative of cannabis, darling," she said faintly. "It's manufactured rather than grown so that the properties can be controlled and various states induced. Right now you're experiencing a time distortion and a sense of superiority. It also has the property of enhancing sensation, more properly your perception of sensation. See?"

She trailed her fingernails across my cheek and it was the most exquisite sensation I'd experienced, scratchy and soft and tingly, as if I could feel each nerve ending exploding and sending a delightful message to my brain. But the pathways to the brain had been shortened miraculously and I could feel the individual explosions instantly.

"Or this," she murmured, and pinched my cheek.

My body bucked and I started to cry immediately, so sharp and hideous was the pain. I controlled my bladder with difficulty and wanted the hurting either to go away or push me over into black oblivion. "Hurting," I moaned through the tears.

"Yes, I expect it does," she said absently. "It's been only eleven minutes since you had the dose. It's a pressure injection gun, much less trouble than a needle, since you don't like our needles. Now let me explain what we are doing." She was brisk and matter-of-fact, unbuttoning my shirt. "It inhibits motor coordination, that's why you are not moving."

She was wrong about the time.

I tried to see her watch, tried to remember when I was sitting there with them, long ago, time was.

She interrupted. "Positive reinforcement is more effective than negative reinforcement. Positive and negative reinforcement combined—the stick and the carrot?—is the most effective of all. I'll tell you this briefly so that you'll have some basis for the . . . horror. To help you understand. Positive reinforcement is the additional ad budget for the new hospital. Congratulations on the new account! Negative reinforcement is the possibility of harm coming to

Tammy—that's long term—and what you're about to experience. The cannabis increases your sensations, your perceptions, while slowing down time for you. The other
compound taps into your particular fear centers, the Gestalt
of those things that frighten you the most. The combination
. . . is most terribly unpleasant."

She injected my arm.

In sixty seconds I would have killed myself had I been
capable of moving enough to chew open a vein. We all
have elemental fears. Heat and cool, black dark and movement at the corners of our consciousness, strange things
crawling, voids of slime erupting puslike forcing facedown
choking breath green itchy pincer cuts, noise, intolerable
noise, burning falling writhing foul monstrosities, shrink-
ing! Pressure bursts eyes. Bowels knotted. Sinus reek.
Mother kills. Falling! Noise.

Suddenly it all cleared. I was guilty. The Court said so,
vague impression of black-robe formalities. I was going to
prison. It was a dream, but more real than any dream I'd
ever experienced. Sweat burst out and I could smell myself.
I knew that I'd be gang-raped in the prison, could feel the
sour breath and see the glittering eyes, had to avoid the
Court's sentence. Flashed to my ex-boss, years ago, shaking
his head, can't help, Beaumont, nothing to be done. But I
can't go to prison. He got a phone call, help me, he was
laughing on the phone, couldn't he see me?

Father there somehow. Looking annoyed. "Do your
time," he said. They'll hurt me there! He turned away.
Wait! They're going to put me in prison, hurt me, raping
pain.

Vince, don't let them. Hector! Wait!

Lots of laughter, hard hands bending back my arms.
Help.

"Not long now," she said.

Drenched in sticky sweat, flowing, pouring from my
skin, foul odor, drowning in it, pumping heart racking my

body, burst of light, pressure. Pressure! "Too much!" I strangled out.

"Hold on, just a moment," she said.

Off table, off, flee, movement impossible, must avoid prison.

I retched violently and Melissa stepped back to avoid the burst of nastiness from my mouth. She looked serene. Even pleased. I smelled myself and it made me sicker.

"If you're through, there's a small bath I'll help you to," she said. "Are you through?"

I lay there and tried to determine if the sensations racing through me were subsiding, and they seemed to be and I croaked something and she waited until I could make myself understood.

"Through," I choked out.

"Take off your clothes and put them in this," she said, handing me a small plastic square. With some effort I unfolded it and it was a steel sack, black and shiny, and some residual fright made me drop it, hurl it away. Jesus God, where had that come from, prison fears and childhood doors bursting open from my unconscious, we never resolve our garbage completely.

"No, no, it's quite all right!" she said impatiently. "It's just a trash sack."

I managed the undressing after a time and struggled to get the ruined clothes into the sack, it twisting and curling away to foul me up like it was alive, and I dropped it violently. She picked it up and held it for me, twisting her face away from the smell and from me.

It took forever to summon up the courage to get into the shower and she had to turn the taps for me, shiny bright chrome, looked hot, but I managed finally, strength barely enough to scrub, and I tottered out after forever and she handed me a huge beach towel and I dried, still supersensitive but controllable.

"That's just a taste. I gave you a hundred milligrams,"

she said. "To approximate schizophrenia, we use three or four times that amount. Not in conjunction with the synthetic cannabis, though, I think that's my unique contribution."

"Psycho . . . psychopharmacology," I said.

"Isn't it wonderful!" She smiled and handed me some nylon coveralls. Good for fishing, dries very quickly, worn mostly by old men with beer cans sitting on the front porch. I put them on, still shaking inside, feeling very old, indeed.

All my life, I've dealt with businesses, understand corporate needs and the people who live the corporate life. All my life.

20

SHE LET ME REST FOR a half hour and then went through a couple of what she called "cognitive tests": name, date, who won the Korean war, name of my mother, afternoon or morning, that sort of thing. Then she advised me to drive very carefully for the next hour or so as my motor reflexes might be a bit impaired. She really didn't seem terribly concerned about it, actually.

I wondered how they had managed, a soundproof conference room? Maybe the yelling had been all in my head? Somehow the horrors were made more horrible by the business setting, the ordinary office, receptionist out front chatting on the phone while brains were being bent inside.

It was out of context as well as out of my experience and the juxtaposition made it worse. I was very anxious to please now, even glad she had found the tape recorder.

"Am I driving somewhere?" I asked. The terrors were leaving me rapidly and I was numbly glad that my mind tended to remember the good and forget the bad. I didn't sleep, though, already I was worried about going to sleep, nightmares. It seemed important to be flip, although it didn't impress her. "Please just listen and listen carefully," she said.

Here is what will happen, she said, cigarette dangling, no attempt to soft-pedal the words, this-is-it-Jack, pay attention, pop quiz, that sort of tone. I would seek an appointment with Dr. Edfelter immediately and reassure him that my paranoid fantasies were either my idea of a bad joke on a woman I had slept with or strictly fantasy. She didn't care which, as long as he was no longer concerned with her or me. "Be convincing, as if your life depended on it," she said. When did I mention Hector? I would forget about Tammy and Tammy's care, which would continue to be provided at B Unit. Tammy was doing well and had shown no interest in resuming our relationship and I would take no further interest in her. "I see no reason we should give up the income from this source," Dr. Stone said. Any further prying by me into the internal affairs of the holding company and Dr. Stone's relationships with patients would be dealt with severely. "I'm speaking of a dosage perhaps twice as strong as you just experienced." If I was tempted to do something reckless, I should remember how easily they had administered the previous paralyzing injection. "It could be administered in your coffee, in a drink, by a person brushing against you in an elevator, please remember that. It could be on your boat, anywhere."

"This is the meeting of minds you mentioned," I said shakily.

"We are actually being more patient with you than normal," she replied. Her eyes were cold and dark. "We gave you a taste of the power, of what can be accomplished, did we not?" How in the hell did I ever go to bed with this reptile? She waited for a smart-ass rejoinder and my mind was a fearful blank so she continued.

I would begin work for the second clinic immediately. They hadn't been joking about that. However, the usual 15 percent commission would be halved, the second half to be mailed to her on a monthly basis as a "finder's fee."

"After all, darling, I found you. Is that not so?" Back to happy, cheerful Melissa. Her character swings were scary in themselves. I tended to believe in the cold-eyed one. Her new kickback probably meant she could redecorate her massive home.

My work would be monitored and if the results were found to be not satisfactory, I could face more chemical difficulties so I had best put forth my strongest efforts. "You have done very well indeed, and this should serve as motivation. Besides which, if the advertising works, we'll increase the budgets and that will profit us both, no?"

"Nobody can guarantee advertising," I protested.

"Darling, you just did," she replied.

Finally, they would leave the commitment order in force, just in case they needed a legal "audit trail." I would sign a standard release form agreeing to clinical testing with experimental compounds. And she handed me the form. I signed with her pen. "That should cover everything," she said briskly.

I wanted to jam the pen in her eye but I signed.

They let me loose after that, I didn't request that my clothes be returned, just the wallet and keys and stuff. The drive home was a nightmare, I couldn't concentrate, crept along, almost missed several red lights. The sign said "Executive Housing." Funny, I didn't feel terribly executive. I showered and showered, mind a near blank, an occasional tremor of fear shaking me. Finally, when the hot water ran out, I got out and went to my hard bed.

No nightmares. Perhaps I'd had my share.

21

Naturally, the work went to hell.

On the surface, everything was the same. I prowled the corridors and made the jokes and did the meetings. I handled the media and placed the ads and met the deadlines, many of which were dictated by dear ol' Horce, who was even more contemptuous than before. He was totally ignorant of what was required, in any advertising area, but made the demands just the same. When I would protest, he said, "Dr. Stone wants it," and laugh.

I was a shaky actor, playing an uncertain role and playing it poorly. At night I plotted and brooded and got nowhere, memories of crawly things and flashes of chemical nightmares clouding my vision. My mood swings were severe, damped by bourbon.

I had more billing (*we* had more billing, Dr. Stone's

greedy mitts were firmly in my pockets; her "share" of the first month's billing would be about three grand) than ever before. Yet the phones weren't ringing when we ran the spots and the reply cards didn't flow in as they did before and the more I struggled with the words and the graphics, the less results I managed to get.

I'd get semi-snide comments tossed in my direction and budgets were closely scrutinized and people complained. Doctors began rewriting my copy, why-can't-you-understand-what-we're-doing-here? and I tried all the tricks I'd learned and nothing worked quite as well as it did before.

The new hospital was a bitch to handle too, geography working against me. The long-distance phone and Federal Express can only do so much.

Melissa didn't ask me to come over, that was a blessing.

And Vince would press me about Tammy and I flared up and we damn near came to blows, so he called and talked to Natelson (whom I had not seen since I slugged him) and apparently was reassured enough to get off my back. Actually I wasn't seeing him just a whole lot and I never told him about Freeport, Melissa, and her magic hypo.

I found myself on the long-distance phone, giving Mrs. Evans a false report on how well Tammy was doing, what did I know? and started crying silently while trying to carry on a conversation with that nice lady.

My Victoria clients went bye-bye, no time for them, and I spent too much effort making their transition to other sources of advertising easy, wanting to give advice and make suggestions and lacking the time to do either coherently. I wondered how the bay house was faring and the poor Grady-White, since I hadn't seen either in more than a month. Untended boats go bad so quickly and I wanted to go to Cuba in mine if I could figure out some way to carry the gas.

I saw Hector as instructed and sat there and lied, eyes

down, until he became annoyed, tore up the bill for the session, and threw me out with instructions to come back when I was willing to work and not insult him with fabrications.

I told myself I was waiting for an opportunity to nail them both, strike at the propitious time, all that. In truth, my will was a touch eroded and the days blended into one another and the time was never right. I could scoot to the bay and forget the works, but disentangling the company from all the relationships and bills due and bills paid and contracts signed, plans made, commitments, insertion orders, and affidavits seemed an impossible task. The issue of Tammy remained, although I got a cheerful report now and again.

And I was afraid.

I drank steadily. Beer in the morning and bourbon at night to the fall-down point. Maybe that had something to do with my noneffective ads, although I suspected a lack of belief in the client. I was a pure-dee mess. On bad nights, I'd wake up at three or four o'clock in the morning and drink some more.

On one of those, a Sunday morning, Vince came bashing at my door with a grim look and a girl in the car. Three-thirty in the morning to be precise, and I was sleeping it off so it took me a long time to get awake and to the door.

"What the fuck you want?" I said blearily.

"We're going fishing," he said. "Get your stuff."

"Screw fishing," I said, and went back toward the bedroom.

I made several steps before he hauled me around and said with no particular emphasis, "We're going fishing, get your stuff."

I looked at him slowly and hangover anger flared inside me and I looked at his eyes and saw he was right.

"Thanks for waking me," I said.

How could he lose the argument? I thought as I struggled into a pair of faded jeans and a pullover a few minutes later. Three o'clock in the morning was Happy Hour for a guy who owned a bar and he didn't have a hangover. Rarely drank too, disgusting. I paused because I thought I'd be sick, no such luck, and then went out to the living area where Vince waited.

"My rods and tackle and stuff are all at the bay."

"Let's go. You need a beer? You look like you need a beer." Although he made his living from drinking, Vince had small patience with drunks.

"I'll take one, maybe for later." In the kitchen I eyed the sadly depleted bourbon bottle and fixed a roadie in a Solo cup. "Hair of the dog," I said over my shoulder to Vince, who was looking disgusted.

Down at the car, the girl was reading by the interior lights, like the kind over your airplane seat, in Vince's big Lincoln towncar. "Beaumont, Kandy. With a 'K,' of course," he said as he started up. "Kandy works for me, just got off." She was petite and cheerful-looking, pert nose, should have freckles although I couldn't tell in this light, and a fluff of blond-brown hair. Good smile.

"Hi, Kandy-with-a-K," I said, and waved my cup.

"You look awful, glad to meet you," she said.

"Beaumont's practically a pro fisherman," Vince said, and accelerated up the freeway ramp to eight-five and set the cruise control. I wondered how many tickets he got and ignored.

Even Vince slowed down in Kendleton. However, I thought we might still set a Houston-to-Point-Lookout world land speed record. The bourbon didn't help and I was sipping cautiously at the not-very-cold beer outside of El Campo. Kandy-with-a-K seemed absorbed in her book and I asked what she was reading.

"It's a book on computer graphics. I'm going to be a

commercial artist when I get through shaking my nekid ass at the geeks."

"We geeks think it's a fine ass, indeed," I replied gallantly. I gathered she was a dancer. Seemed well up on the high end, brains-wise. It was odd for Vince to socialize with one of his dancers, but I never could figure out what Dr. Stone would call his "sexuality." Once he had a near-teeny-bopper living with him and a couple of times he went on an extended vacation with an elegant lady who was close to a superb fifty.

"Kandy's one of the few who might do it too," Vince said sourly. It was his first conversation for forty miles. He tends to crush and spindle social niceties. I was used to it and it didn't seem to bother Kandy, who smiled over the backseat and went back to her book.

Thirty miles farther we turned at Ganado and headed for the bay. Vince said into the silence of the car, "I can't help you being an asshole."

I was three-quarters asleep and mumbled and Kandy asked, "Is it a woman? You look like a guy who gets fucked up over women."

"Don't we all?"

"I don't," Vince said.

"But women are your commodity, baby," Kandy said reasonably. "Would a rancher get fucked up over his cows? Beaumont looks like a romantic."

"I can have relationships," Vince said, offended.

"On your terms and by your rules. Not that you aren't sweet and quite nice," Kandy said, and I choked quietly. Vince and sweet seemed diametrically opposed but maybe she knew.

"Not that I have, want, or will have any firsthand knowledge," she said to me reassuringly, and he snorted.

Tactfully I asked about her commercial art background and she told me she was in her third semester at the Art Institute and the tuition was a killer and she was dancing her way through school. "I rather like the sound of that," she said. "Although the reality is not quite so . . . fluffy."

"Your body is your edge, so you use it. Dumb not to," Vince said flatly.

"Bring your portfolio around sometime and I'll look at it," I said offhandedly.

"Thanks," she replied. "But I think I'll wait till I find somebody with real interest." Vince glanced at me in the mirror and I could read his eyes in the dark. What was so wrong with what I said?

He said, "Let's hear about your tough time."

"Which one?"

"Don't be flip. Talk."

"I don't want to bore Kandy-with-a-K," I said, and she flipped her hand, don't-mind-me, and went on reading.

"Talk," Vince said again, and I stared at him. For the most private human being I'd ever met to ask me to discuss personal business in front of a third party was incomprehensible. "Kandy's smart and she keeps her mouth shut and you can talk, so talk," he said shortly.

"Kandy's got to pee so if you'll find me a service station, Mr. Beaumont can get started without me," she said.

"Hey," I said, leaning up on the back of the front seat. "I didn't mean to start a war. If I was impolite or rude or both, I apologize." She looked at me for a minute and Vince swerved the car toward an exit and an all-night filling station, which threw her close to me, and she peck-kissed my nose, rather an odd gesture.

"Forgiven," she said, and kissed my nose again. I had never thought of the nose as an erogenous zone. Maybe there was hope for me yet.

"Girl's got a nose fetish, Vince," I said.

He slammed the big car to a stop by the pumps and she said, "Nasal sodomy's my game," and got out for the

Ladies. I wouldn't get the head start on True Confessions because I needed the Men's.

The peculiar green-gray light of a smelly highway gas station rest room did little for my self-esteem as I looked in the mirror. On the wall, somebody had been kind enough to report one of the local ladies shaved her pubic hair.

22

So I TOLD THEM, shaving words and inflections, omitting a bit here and there, slanted reporting but who would not in these circumstances? Everything: money, Dr. Stone, her steamy relationship group, the videotape, B Units, my inadvertent spell of drug addiction, escape, and how I managed to get them really mad at Don Nelson's office. The nightmare chemicals. Plus the terms under which I was working. I made myself sound as good as possible, which may have been a lost cause. Even so, it was not a very flattering portrait of the post-Tammy Beaumont, and I paused for a minute when I realized that was an accurate description. I was all alone. Again.

"Fuck," said Vince.

Kandy had put away her book and hung over the back of the front seat a little, sympathetic, her eyes kind in the thin light in the car. It was still that peculiar expectant dark before the sky lightens in the east with morning thunderclouds silhouetted and a touch pink and we were ripping down F.M. 172 and I wondered idly if the boat battery was down.

"It's slavery," she said. She was kind enough not to add a less-than-flattering description of the slave. I wondered why I was standing still for the treatment I'd described, a chemical residue from the stuff they'd shot me with? Or just a plain ol' character flaw? Have to check Hector, consult my aged *PDR*.

"Well, I've been waiting to—" I began, and Vince interrupted.

"You been bending over so as to give them just the right angle to ream you. Shit. I don't even want to fish with you."

"It could be the chemicals. You don't know, Vince." Kandy was quick in my defense and I was grateful to the point of tears.

"I didn't ask for you to come waking me up, pal," I said, and it would have been stronger except there was a quaver in my voice because I knew he was right and loathed myself.

"Look, Beaumont, you're fairly weird and you run around too much beating up on yourself, but you've never been a wimp. Even when you had trouble, you were thinking your way out. Always. And, shit! You could laugh at it. Now you're whining and hiding. Shit. Gimme a cigarette."

"You don't smoke."

"Gimme."

"I want to fish with you," Kandy said, and patted my hand. My sex appeal seemed to evoke maternal instincts in strange ladies. I handed Vince a cigarette and he punched in the lighter on the dash.

"Hope you choke," I said.

*   *   *

The boat was stuck on the trailer. Let five thousand pounds sit too long and the fiberglass and rubber rollers on which it sits become very friendly. In the end we had to float it off and yank it off with near full throttle in reverse from the twin Yamahas on the stern, Vince's big car backed down the ramp until salt water was lapping at his bumper.

The engines coughed and spit and stumbled and a friendly spider had woven a fine web on the bowrail and Kandy had the good sense to stand aside holding the bowline while Vince and I yelled at each other. I let the engines run enough to clear up, bursts of throttle briefly in neutral and wiped down everything, sloshed a couple of buckets of salt water over the deck to clean off some of the debris, and we were off.

The mosquitoes and sand fleas were in stern competition and I rummaged until I found some Deep Woods Off! and gave it to Kandy so the paying customers wouldn't have to overlook bites on her epidermis while they lusted in their hearts on her next professional appearance. It was a fine epidermis, what I could observe, blouse tied across a flat midriff, shapely legs protruding from her bikini. I let Vince suffer.

Maybe the bugs would be afraid to bite his grumpy ass.

But we got organized and away in good time, order restored on twenty-five feet of Grady-White, beer and soft drinks in the cooler, several dozen skittering brown shrimp in the live well for bait, rods in the vertical holders on the gunwales, gray light showing me the way out of the slip, a slight coolness in the air, and I felt fine through my hangover. I punched up the engines and they steadied into a satisfactory roar.

"Hope you've got some long pants," I hollered to Kandy.

"You're the first one to tell me to 'put it on, put it on,' actually. But I do," she hollered back.

Vince, up in the bow, waved me onward. Fish awaiting.

*　　*　　*

The twenty-five-foot Grady-White is too big a boat for successful bay fishing, especially in the shallows and oyster reefs where the speckled trout and redfish roam. So we parked the boat on the beach at Sand Point (every bay in America has at least one Sand Point) and got out to wade. Vince had a store-bought wade-fisherman's belt with loops, straps, attachments, and pockets for knives and pliers and the works. I stuck a stainless pair of needlenose pliers in my pocket, looped a stringer around my waist, and played Teacher with Kandy. I wished it were Doctor.

"Wade with me, that way we'll both use the same bait bucket. You hook the shrimp like this and you toss it out and pop the cork. Fish hear the sound and think it's another fish and come over to investigate. Greedy creatures, fish. You keep your thumb on the reel like this so you don't backlash."

She nodded, hooked a shrimp expertly, and flipped the rig maybe a hundred twenty feet away. Clicked the reel back into gear and popped the cork. "You're talking to a Laguna Madre girl," she said. "I love to fish, my daddy taught me. That's why I got Vince to bring me, when I heard . . . he's real worried about your . . . you."

"Right," I said. "Right. If I make any serious errors in technique, let me know, okay?" Then I cast and caught the wind just right and managed to beat her effort by five feet, for which I was silently grateful.

We caught a spec or three, a couple of slime-festooned gafftop, one nice red that took a bunch of line away and splashed and thrashed in a satisfactory fashion, and missed the usual number of monsters, all of which would have been state records. By eleven o'clock we gathered back at the boat, stinging from the sun and ready for a legitimate beer.

Kandy doffed her wading clothes and stretched out on

the bow in her bikini and I had a hard time not leering. Vince gave her a professional inspection and talked about the jetties, should we maybe run to Pass Cavallo, go out and anchor in the surf, soak some mullet around the deep holes.

I opted to run back in and fry a fish for lunch and maybe take a nap, wouldn't that be nice and air conditioned.

Which we did, if I would run to the pass on the evening tide.

With boat-washing and fish-cleaning chores, the obligatory visit to the Evanses' and this and that, it was dark again when we finally headed home. No tarpon in the pass, although we looked, and Kandy tanned rather than burned, not bad for a blonde. Perhaps her breasts didn't meet skin-magazine standards but she was altogether a well-found wench and I could see why she was a featured performer at Vince's.

She caught the most and biggest fish too.

In the car, cruise control set at a leisurely seventy-five, Vince said, "I was scared once when I was a kid. Tony Lopez."

"Who?"

"Tony Lopez, a Mexican kid I went to school with. He was the pitcher on the ninth-grade team. He had grown up faster than we did, almost six feet then, and he was the pitcher. Threw so hard I just stood there with the bat on my shoulder, hoping he wouldn't hit me. Frozen. Finally, I realized I had to do something or he'd keep throwing too fast right by me. Maybe hit me. So I stuck the bat out and got a hit, completely by chance because my eyes were shut closed."

There was a silence. This might have been the longest uninterrupted speech I'd ever heard from him. "Proving?" I asked.

"You got to do something or sooner or later he'll bean you."

"I love parables," Kandy said.

When we got to my place, I invited them in for a drink.

"No," said Vince.

"Sure," said Kandy.

He shrugged, stuck his hand out to shake, and told me to behave myself. "You need anything . . ." he said.

So the two of us walked into my impersonal housing and I mixed her a bourbon on the rocks, had a glass myself, and we talked for about three hours until I realized how late it was and offered to run her home.

"Why?" she asked, and I couldn't think of a single good reason. I fixed another drink, realizing it was just my second and her glass was still half full although the ice cubes had melted until the mix was bourbon-flavored water.

"I'm going to shower," she said. "Want to join me?"

I did. Badly needed a shower. I couldn't think of anything I needed more, ever. I was grateful for a large-capacity water heater.

Later I was reminded of Tammy early on and started to choke up about it, told her, told her bluntly what I feared, and she hugged and patted until the spell had past.

"Nothing's guaranteed, even when it's guaranteed," she said. "Might as well enjoy what is for what it is, huh?"

"On a scale of ten, you broke the meter."

"It's the salt water. Always makes me horny."

23

WE WENT TO THE MOVIES and held hands. I found she was a sucker for a backrub and she showed me that most of my tension was in my feet although why anybody would want to rub my beat-up corn-infested feet was beyond me.

She made me take her to a Japanese restaurant and I discovered Rumaki and we went to obscure subtitled movies at the Greenway that she insisted would improve my mind. I introduced her to the Travis McGee books in retaliation and she was lost to me for an entire weekend. Bullit liked her.

I went through her portfolio and showed her what to eliminate and what a studio or agency would be looking for, suggested that she form a habit of doing absurdly neat production art, and gave her a job or two to design for me.

Which I paid for at the going rates although she thought that was too much.

One night I went to Vince's and watched her dance and hated it, wanted to punch out one particularly obnoxious shouting customer and blind the rest. Vince stopped me from being an ass, cut off the loudmouth's drinks, which made him leave, and took me into the back and poured me a drink of the good stuff.

"That's nothing," he said. "Nothing. It's what she does to get the bread. She doesn't trick and didn't before she met you and who are you to be such a prude anyway? I've seen you out there with your tongue hangin' out."

"True. Too true."

"Hey. Your famous lecture about two independent people . . . persons . . . choosing to be together and letting each other do their thing? Live it."

"You said that was shit."

"It is." He grinned. "Now you get to live it."

Outside there was a moderate roar and a lot of clapping and I wished she'd get the hell off the stage. I didn't want to think about the traditional tuck-the-buck in the G-string game.

"Tammy's out," Vince said, looking intently at me.

"She is?"

"Yeah. Last week. She asked me to give you this."

It was a note, typical Tammy with little circles for the dots over the "i's," lots of swashy character in uppercase letters, she'd always love me but she didn't love me, Dr. Natelson had helped her see the unhealthiness of our relationship, besides there was someone in Group that she was interested in, she would never forget me and would Mrs. Evans pack up her clothes and mail them to the new address below.

"San Antonio?"

"That's what she said. She's still about ten pounds light to my eye but she looks a whole lot better than she did."

He looked at me steadily. How could she dump me so easily? I was suddenly bone-afraid and I didn't know why. I'd been alone before. Tammy and I were a done deal, I knew that.

"I don't really feel, she really should have, shit!"

"Lose one, gain one," said Vince.

"That's not the way it is, Vince."

"I know that," he said seriously. "But it's what you gotta say. Kinda means the lady-doc has lost her grip on your balls, though."

"Yeah," I said. "Yeah, it does. But I still feel like your proverbial reject." That's why I was afraid. My excuse had gone to San Antonio. Vince kept looking at me. Somewhere, deep down, I could feel happiness like a glow. "Yeah," I said. "It does."

"Absolutely not!" said Dr. Stone. "There is no way I'll even consider it." In a nonsubtle body-language gesture, she lighted a cigarette and swiveled her chair around so her back was to me.

"Things change, Melissa," I said, trying to watch around me in a 360-degree circle.

"This is not one of them. Besides, you can't afford to quit."

"I'll make do."

"I forbid it!"

"Look, lady," I said, standing up. "You can forbid all you fuckin' well want but I'm what you call your history. I'm gone, vanished, bye-bye. You can take your accounts and your kickbacks and all your scams and shove them, assuming your saggy ass isn't occupied otherwise." It wasn't saggy but I thought the physical insult might get the point across. I liked the way I sounded. Tough and sure. Appearances are everything.

"My dear Beaumont," she said, turning back to me. Damn, she was staggering. This was sweet Melissa, not brisk Dr. Stone or wicked Melissa the Witch. "We have been through a great deal together and . . . perhaps I have not been as attentive as I should have been. Remember?"

"No thanks," I said flatly. "I quit. I've told the media and I've settled up the bills. Your accounting department has been a little bit too efficient paying me, so I'm not hanging out anywhere. I've told everybody to bill you direct from now on."

"Marketing is not a function or a responsibility I care to take on. How can you give up this income?"

"I just did. Footloose and fancy-free, that's me."

"You fool! You'll never find anyone like me. Or an account this large. You'll be ruined."

"I've *been* ruined, Melissa. You may have noticed."

"We have been very good for each other," she said, moving closer. We were in her office, the TV blank although I could visualize some patients performing for her and her current consort(s) unknowingly. I shuddered. She was a remarkable woman, pulsing with energy, undeniably attractive even now, but I kept remembering her cold voice and the clear liquid in the hypo. "I have some new things to show you, perhaps tonight? Then we could discuss . . ."

"No. I have a date. We have nothing to discuss. I'll see you," I said, and started to get up.

"Wait just a moment, damn you!"

I paused at the door. She settled herself behind the desk. "It is a matter of business," she said. "I simply cannot afford to let you resign. I would be uneasy forever."

"Because of the 'alphabet units' and a little drugging here and there? Why would that worry you, Melissa?" I was quite proud of my rehearsed mannerisms and style. Vince had offered off-handedly to sit in on the meeting, and that was an affront to whatever pride I had left. So I had practiced. So far, I was getting eights and nines from the row of invisible judges. No applause in the head yet, not till I got out of here.

"Everything is perfectly legal!"

"Of *course* it is," I said brightly. "So you have nothing to worry about, right?" I came back to her desk. "You have nothing to worry about from me, I 'don't want to get involved.' But you know it can't go on forever, somebody's gonna blow the whistle. But it won't be me, so let's forget it, okay?"

"You talk too much," she said to me. Then, almost to herself: "Your male ego will ultimately not be able to stand it and you will try some foolish scheme to avenge it. And that I will not have." She looked at me coldly. "You do remember your hospitalizations? I believe you are becoming dangerous to yourself and others again. Yes."

"Don't start that shit again," I replied, trying to keep my voice calm. "Several other people know about your tricky chemicals and why I'm here. I'm no threat." Believe me, crazy person.

"Run along, darling, and enjoy yourself. Perhaps there may have to be almost an epidemic of mental disease in your circle."

"Don't push, Melissa. You can't drug the whole world. And Tammy's gone away, so that lever is gone."

"Yes," she said absently. "As one tool becomes useless, you seek a new one. The child's name is Kandy, is it not?" Her eyes had that glittery look again. I got the hell out of there, making sure nobody got close to me as I left.

How in the hell did she know about Kandy?

"We're leaving and we're not coming back and you can forget the Art Institute and Vince and those creeps who stuff money in your pants!" I was yelling, and Kandy flinched.

"I can't, Beaumont. It's what I do for now and I make good money and I'm not coming down to sponge off of you!"

"It's not sponging!"

"She's just bluffing, she's gotta be."

"She's about semicrazy and I 'know too much,' which is corny but true."

"Baby, baby. You've quit and we'll both be careful and she'll forget all about us in a couple of weeks. She'll get somebody new to do her ads and run her scams and shit, not to worry. Besides which, what do you care?"

"I care. Damn. Can't you tell I care?"

"I mean about the creeps. As long as it's only money in my pants, what do you care?" She grinned and kissed my nose. "I've got to go to work, we'll finish talking about it later."

"But . . ." I sputtered and she waved and was gone. I poured myself a drink, remembering that my liquor store bill was practically nonexistent these days, and went back to my packing. Kandy would just have to take her act on the road, as far away as possible. She could work for me. Victoria had three topless clubs, as far as that goes, if she insisted on working her profession.

I felt a bit pimpy, but I could learn to handle it.

At eleven that night Vince called and asked why she hadn't come to work.

24

O<small>H, GOD *DAMN*,</small>" I said aloud.

Then I dialed Melissa's home phone and she answered on the second ring.

"This was a big mistake, Melissa. I meant what I said . . . about no threat."

"Could we not have a pleasantry or two first, darling? How have I been, what has been happening, who am I sleeping with?"

"Immaterial and I have zero interest in the above. Have you shot her full of that shit?"

"You are referring to the young lady with the absurd name? A trifle . . . nonabundant for your tastes I would have thought."

"Skip the fun and games. Have you used that shit on her?"

"Actually, no. A mild sedative only. She's sleeping quite peacefully at the clinic. In one of the locked wards, of course, we wouldn't want her to make an unauthorized exit, against medical advice, would we?"

"Okay. This was a mistake but we don't have to make it into a nuclear event. I'll go get her and bring her home and we'll forget it, okay?"

"I had an exchange planned." Somebody was pounding on my door, Vince.

"If you think I'm going back into the hospital where you can play games with my brain, you need to examine your reality base, Dr. Stone."

"It wasn't that bad, darling."

"Worse. Forget it. I'll have every law enforcement authority in the area out there before daybreak if you don't knock it off."

"These would be the same persons who are looking for an escaped patient, one from the locked wards? One whose commitment order is still in effect?"

"Let me think about it," I said, and hung up.

Vince was doing his level best to knock the door down. I yelled for him to hold it and let him in.

"She's got Kandy and she wants to swap."

"For you?"

"Yep. Little ol' me."

"You sure can pick 'em, Beaumont." Then he looked at me and waited.

"How do you feel about a little felony tonight, Vince?"

"Hell, it's a full moon, let's do it."

"Just don't let anybody stick you with a hypo or you'll be baying at it."

"I'm scared of shots anyway."

I had Vince drive to Melissa's home in the Blazer, although I wondered if the sturdy four-wheel drive could adapt to his driving style. When we got there, I sent him around back of the two-story structure to wait. The kitchen entry was out there.

"Try not to rouse the neighbors," I offered, and he grunted.

Then I went to the front and leaned on the doorbell.

"Beaumont, what a nice surprise." She was back in her canvas-looking shorts and a top and I remembered silver tarpon glinting. The door was on a sturdy chain. "I take it you've agreed to the exchange I mentioned?"

"I need specifics. You going to let me in?"

"Please understand that violence will gain you nothing—perhaps a momentary satisfaction—but then the reaction on your friend will also be violent. What do you see in that scrawny child?"

"I see no videotapes, mostly." That really wasn't right, I liked dirty movies and nastiness and everything you could do. But Kandy was real and Melissa made me act. Or something.

"A puritan at heart." She sneered and let me in.

"I need a drink," I said. "Can I go back and fix it before we talk?"

"Of course. Bring me some Smirnoff, please."

I made the drinks, let Vince in, raised the bottle to see if he wanted a pop, and he shook his head "no" violently and motioned me to hurry.

I went back to the living room, one of the few times we'd used it, gave her the drink and slumped on the couch. "None of this was necessary or clever," I said. "I wouldn't have . . . I have no burning desire to upset whatever applecarts you've got going."

"But how could I know?"

"You're a shrink, can't you tell when I tell the truth?"

"It sounds that way, darling. But I've been fooled so many times. I need to be sure. The business with the girl is just to make a point, we have no interest in her."

"No B Unit for Kandy, huh?"

"Do you realize we now have five of the special units? The return is quite fantastic and I just can't have it upset."

"So what's the deal?" How do you congratulate somebody on a successful fraud? Way to go, you've ripped off another five mil?

"We will continue on as before. You will handle our marketing and continue to serve both hospitals. I suppose my percentage of your income could increase . . . but we can discuss that later." She had the coy sureness of someone whose hand is on the switch. The switch controls the electrical current to your testicles.

"And you'll keep your mitts off of Kandy."

"Of course!"

"Not good enough," said Vince from the door, and he walked over and slapped the shit out of her. Drink went flying, ice cubes on the rug, and she sat down hard on the floor, with the chair arm underneath her. She looked stunned. I *was* stunned. Lawsuits, police, violence in the streets. I was well over my head with no time to rehearse.

He picked her up with one hand and righted the chair with the other. "You shouldn't mess around with people, except like you're supposed to," he told her. He acted as though beating on noted doctors was run of the mill. I wished I were elsewhere until I remembered Kandy.

"I'm trying to remember the last time I've been struck," she said, wondering. The lady was cool, I'll give her that. I wonder what background she came from. Maybe getting slapped around was a new thrill. I had about as much knowledge of Melissa's inner thought processes as I did of a spider's. Just the same, I was glad Vince had popped her, not me. This makes me either sensible or a coward or both.

"The next time is right around the corner," I said, sick but hiding it. Vince was a touch direct for my taste and this situation. Maybe he liked to negotiate from strength.

"We want the girl back here now," he said.

"And if I don't, you'll beat up on me until I do. I know we saw this on television. Darling, does he mean it?"

Before I could answer he knocked her off the chair again. Solid blows, open hand, not bone crunchers but enough to move her not-inconsiderable weight off the chair.

"He means it."

"Very well," she said from the floor. "No further demonstrations needed. I'll have Kandy back here in the morning."

"You'll call right now," Vince said quietly, "to whoever's on duty and tell them Beaumont will pick her up in . . . an hour?"

"I can get there in an hour easy," I said. "What you going to do in the meantime?"

"I'll think of something," he said, staring at Dr. Stone.

"I could call the police," she said.

"If we'd let you," he said flatly. They played Eyeball. "And," he added, "the first question they'd ask is 'Why were they beating up on you, Doctor?' And you'd say something and we'd say a whole lot of things and everything would get confused. Maybe make the papers. You don't really want that."

She looked a little dazed but still very handsome. Both cheeks were red where he had slapped her and I remembered my mother telling me about pinching her cheeks when she was a child, no makeup allowed, to get a healthy color. Could we sell Vince as the Ultimate Cosmetic?

She went to the phone and called, Vince right beside her. When she was through, he nodded to me, took her arm quite gallantly, and escorted her to the couch. "May I get you another drink?" he asked politely. "Maybe some wine?"

I missed her reply because I was worrying that she had given some code words and I would be snagged with a net the minute I hit the hospital grounds. "About two, two and a half hours, Vince," I said.

"We'll be here."

Melissa said something about "elemental" and I left. Vince was lighting her Winston like a gentleman and she was looking at him as intently as I did.

There wasn't any trouble at the hospital, as if a wee-hours checkout happened all the time. I signed an insurance form and reflected that Dr. Stone had refined the art of kidnapping: the victim had to pay for the privilege. Kandy was a sleepy child against my shoulder as I drove home through the early-morning fog. Vince answered the door at Melissa's house with a vastly self-satisfied look.

"Want some breakfast?" he asked as he got into the back. "JoJo's is good this time of night. Lots of freaks and weirdos and plain ol' drunk ladies."

25

I HAD $22,000 and change in the bank. For me this was wealth. Maybe not beyond the dreams of avarice, but wealth. It represented my net profits, April 15th would be a killer, from marketing two hospitals for a number of months and I skipped the last payment to Dr. Stone. So I had money. And a good thing too, I was having a heap of trouble scraping up an income. It seems Victoria business has a long memory and had no intention of giving me work when I might run off the next time a big Houston client beckoned.

So the money was a nice cushion, although it wouldn't last all that long. Filling up my boat was a plus—one-hundred-dollar experience and live bait shrimp cost nine dollars a quart. I'm not sure how the quart system for bait evolved, and the containers they used to measure (old green bean cans sewed into the bottom of a dipnet) didn't look like quart-size to me.

Kandy, however, was doing famously.

Her predictable outrage had been muted considerably when I outlined the perfectly legal method Dr. Stone had used to commit me and my brief description of some of the creepy-crawly chemical available had scared her silly. At breakfast that morning Vince and I had listened to a lot of "She can't do this!" and "We have to tell somebody!" until we pointed out that a topless dancer and friends had little philosophical clout when compared to a noted member of the medical establishment.

"We're winners. Don't fuck with it," Vince had advised.

So she agreed to go lay in the metaphorical weeds with me.

The hospital abduction had sobered her somewhat although she insisted on applying successfully at Peaches, Victoria's finest gentleman's club, situated in a Quonset hut out the highway from Ganado, with a parking lot full of pickups on Friday and Saturday nights.

"Cowboys are quite polite until they figure you've made a deal, Beaumont," she observed. "Then it takes a sledge to fend them off. And I wish they'd take off their hats once in a while. Did you know that messing with a hat is a fightin' offense? And no, I'm not making any deals. Some sunbitch tipped me a quarter, can you believe that?"

She was a star of sorts, I gathered.

I refused to go look at her, remembering how I felt the one time I'd seen her dance at Vince's, even though the country stripper costumes were somewhat more modest. I kept seeing cowboy hands, fat and callused and approximating the ham of a pig, with greasy dollar bills.

Kandy insisted on sharing the household expenses, which was a switch. Her commercial art career was sidetracked for the moment, although she did do some paste-ups for me and the fall fishing was rather splendid, the fish population recovering from a massive freeze kill-off in the early 80s.

So why did I insist on upsetting such a placid applecart?

Hey, it's much more fun to do advertising when you have money to play with. And can buy broadcast media, meet with producers, check computer printouts of reach and frequency, make analyses, play with the big boys. There were bigger boys yet, in New York and maybe Los Angeles, but Houston was big enough to be interesting. And my health care ads had worked. I had started on a bit of a reputation, Beaumont is Back!, a little noise in the trade press, all good for the ego, praise for your very own ads. Mostly, they had worked.

It's very nice to see tangible results from work you did, the phones ringing, smiles on the face of the admissions director, five- and six-figure checks. And your effort is the same: whether you're spending a hundred bucks running two column by five in the *Victoria Advocate* or eighty thousand on a TV buy to be viewed by three hundred thousand people.

So I put together a sample ad package, veloxes and cassette tapes and a short résumé, and sent it to four hospitals much in the same line of work as Melissa's group. I needed the biz.

"You're asking for trouble," Kandy said.

But we hadn't heard "boo" from Dr. Stone and she had plenty of time to get hostile if she wished, so why not? I couldn't base all the rest of my life on what now felt like merely an unpleasant experience. The mind is a wonderful thing.

I got two calls from my solicitation package within a week. One marketing lady wanted to shave commissions and fees before we were six minutes into a discussion of what I might be able to do for her hospital. Much like shopping with coupons, I guess, but I told her I wouldn't play that way. The other guy was interested and we made an appointment for a Monday.

"The whole mess is going to start up again," Kandy said, and wandered off to the park and the concrete bulkhead. I found her there two hours later, just watching the bay, and gave her a hug.

"Not to worry, sleeping dogs and so forth," I said.

"It's going to be bad," she said flatly.

"Weren't you the lady who wanted revenge? This way I'll steal all Dr. Stone's customers and hit her in her pocketbook."

She shrugged.

I made the deal with the second hospital, two meetings in Houston feeling like a fugitive, no overnights, a quick drink at Vince's and some fish-lies and hit the highway. Everybody missed Kandy, he assured me, and I grimaced.

"You trained her well, she's knockin' them dead in Victoria, Vince."

"Maybe it's just a phase. Get her pregnant." He grinned at my horror at the thought.

"She's making twice as much as I have been."

"So what? Aren't you a secure man of the eighties?"

"My metaphysical growth stopped in April of 1969, I think."

And when I got home from the second meeting at the hospital, where we made the deal, Kandy was waiting scared shitless.

"She called. Goddamn it, I told you."

"Who?" I asked although I knew.

"Dr. Stone, she's going to get us, why did you . . . why couldn't you listen to me!"

"Jealous, no doubt, since I'm about to ace her out, market-share-wise," I said with more confidence than I felt. I looked at my bourbon glass suspiciously. In the boat, at my house, in an elevator, Melissa had said. Anywhere. Just a little dab will do ya, went through my head.

"Call her and tell her you've changed your mind. Please?"

"Jesus, Kandy! I need the business and I'm no threat to her. She probably just wants to . . ." I didn't know what the hell she wanted to talk to me about.

So I called. And got the good Dr. Stone, whose secretary now answered the phone with a title. Maybe Melissa was going up in her world. Just shows you what chicanery, double-dealing, confidence games can do for a girl.

"Beaumont, you have a penchant for irritating me," she said without preamble.

"Not intentional. You're a page from the past."

"I wish to leave it that way. Not have you back in Houston, especially when I need . . . especially when I gave you the opportunity to . . . I showed you—"

Through her sputtering I finally determined that she felt herself wronged, which must have taken a nimble bit of mental gymnastics. Her counterparts had apparently contacted her for references. And that her continued "good performance" admissions-wise had put her in line for the job of spokesperson for a national psychiatric association, stepping-stone to the presidency, a position that meant she'd be consulted by the White House Committee on Mental Health if there was one. The White House has never been a bastion of mental health, I thought. She should have just stiffed me on the recommendations, we all know how. Inflection, a pause allowed to linger too much, half-finished sentences, you can nail a guy and never say anything that could be used against you. Naturally, I had to wise off.

"Hell, Melissa, you can tell 'em how to save money on hospitalization by leaving out the hospitalization," I remarked.

"Any problems now, anything connected with me,

would be exceedingly poor timing," she said. No rising inflection, she flat meant it.

"You could publish your psychopharmacological experiments, willing subjects versus a control group you kidnapped," I suggested.

"Don't come to Houston," she said.

"Please? Pretty please? How about 'Unknowing Aphrodisiacs, The Use of Patients in Porno Tapes,' that's a good one," I said into a stony silence.

"You heard me," she replied, and slammed the phone down.

"Not to worry," I said to Kandy. "We've got her on the run."

26

"POISONING AT TOPLESS CLUB!" screamed the headline in the venerable *Houston Post* two days later. I did a comic take when I saw the headline, neck muscles suddenly tight. The story underneath was nicely absent of leers although the reporter did note that several of the girls attracted quite a crowd as they were carried out.

Vince had handled the problem well, calling 911 and some doctor customers when the first patron went bonkers and there were no fatalities although he was closed while the health inspectors when through his kitchens and bar with the well-known fine-tooth comb. For a toxin that made some people act crazy and others to turn zombie. Lots of luck.

He made the AP wire and they spelled the name right, although Foxy Lady is not much of an achievement.

Jesus, I bet he's mad, was my first thought. Then I hoped he wasn't mad at me, please god. Then I tried to convince myself it was food poisoning and resolved not to drink from anything but sealed containers. But wasn't it an umbrella they nailed that guy in London, the spy, with? I couldn't stay away from everybody, forever. Why couldn't I leave well enough, so forth.

It was eight-thirty in the evening and I was on my deck reading the early edition of the *Post*, which some poor soul delivered in the wee hours to the hinterlands. Kandy was off doing her first set. My campaign for the big new hospital ("Drunks Have All the Fun" with a photo of a blood-smeared guy in a suit that I had picked up from a photographer's "Grim File" for 350 bucks) had been approved and I was down to about fifteen grand.

It couldn't be. Surely.

Evans drove up in the omnipresent pickup and honked. I went to the railing to lean down. "They want you to call them in Victoria, at the club," he said with a grimace. The Evanses had not got over Tammy although they were polite to my new roomie. "And did you say some fella could use your boat? Ugly little bastard?"

"Okay and no," I said.

"Thought so. I ran him off. Use the phone at the house, you want. Mamma's in the garden." He waved and drove off. Mamma's in the garden and therefore can't be corrupted by a call to a topless club. Who was messin' with the boat?

I decided to call the club first, the awesome power of the phone, and the manager said Kandy was drunk and would I please come get her, if she was going to act this way, yak yak. "Twenty minutes," I said, and hung up.

Kandy drank like the minister drank. Kandy didn't like the taste or the effects. Kandy saw too many drunks to be one. I had told him to absolutely under no circumstances let her leave and was in the Blazer driving like Vince toward Victoria inside of a minute. Kandy didn't drink, that was the whole of it. The Blazer has the big V-8 and I kept the back two barrels of the carb open much of the way, whipping past pickups with gunracks, swaying hard on the high-crown country roads.

"Maybe I shouldn't have told her she couldn't drug the whole world," I said to Bullit, who was in her high-G posture on the back deck, paws braced and spread, eyes bright.

Exciting, oh boy!

Kandy was damn near comatose, except for a giggle now and again. She kept trying to show us her breasts, us being me and the manager who was a fairly nice guy and seemed a bit embarrassed by the whole thing. "We tell them not to drink the customers' drinks, to stick to the sugar-water stuff we mix 'em," he said apologetically.

"It won't happen again." And I hoisted her up, found her street clothes, and got her into them more or less and left. I didn't let anybody get close to me as I three-quarters carried her out. The customers made jokes and I almost set her down to explain the need for politeness but I couldn't fight and watch her at the same time.

On the way back, she kept asking me what happened and giggling. Then she got suddenly sad and began to cry hopelessly. Then she passed out and I drove the last fifteen miles with my hand on her neck, feeling her pulse, to make sure it was a pass-out. Kandy was so controlled, aware and finely tuned, that it was terrifying to see her sloppy and weird.

Bullit put her face on her paws and wiggled away to the far corner of the rear deck, nervous and whiny, wanting to get away from the rage that was coming off me.

Kandy's pulse was fine and she was breathing fine so I didn't call the doctor. Then I worried about that, although my choices weren't all that great: a semiretired general practitioner who lived up the road and was nuts about floundering and the emergency room in Port Lavaca, where they didn't see too much in the way of exotic compounds.

I checked her every fifteen minutes, sleeping in our bed with a sad smile. Girl should know better than to get involved with me. The bitch. Melissa, not Kandy. I nursed a drink, no wrecks needed if we had to make a run to the hospital, and in a couple of hours she looked better and seemed to be sleeping normally.

I sat on the deck and plotted in the night.

"It was a bug," she said at the breakfast table. I was late for the drive to Houston: media and budget for the new campaign. "She wouldn't and couldn't do anything to us down here."

"Repeat after me: stay here, drink out of sealed cans, eat out of sealed cans, and I'll be back at eight or so."

"Sure. Can I take the boat up the crik?"

"Creek. And no. I don't trust the boat."

She got up and gave me a laughing hug. "Beaumont, if you don't trust the boat there's no hope for you. I won't hurt your precious boat."

"Evans said somebody was messing with it."

And that quieted her down, tightened her lips, and made her nod. "Maybe I'll go visit Mrs. Evans."

"Cans. Remember: cans."

I whipped through the two-hour drive to Houston, was brusque but successful at my meeting, called Vince and found no news and maybe they'd let him open in two more days. No lawsuits yet but he and his insurance company were braced.

"You think it's the bitch," he said, no question in his voice. "Maybe I'll pay her a little visit."

"Maybe it worked momentarily before, but I suspect she's covered that possibility, don't you?"

"Let's go look."

"I'll do it if I can be home by eight or so."

"Jesus, Beaumont, you can't handle shit like this if you've got to be home before dark!" But he agreed to let me pick him up and we cruised the Tanglewood house. Two dark cars, blackwall tires, off-duty cops I thought.

"They've got us outnumbered," I said on the second pass.

"This may be a way of life," he grumbled. "So what are you going to do? I can wait."

"Finesse."

"One of your strong points, I've noticed."

"Also carefully crafted lies. I'm good at lies."

And he looked at me and nodded, which I thought a testimonial of a sort. I headed for the bay, leaving him to his grumbling.

What'd he mean, I was good at lies?

It took me a long time, working against the fading light, to check the boat. Outboard-powered boats are probably about as safe a watercraft as you can get and a good thing too, considering some of the bonehead stunts I'd witnessed. I'd once watched a fiberglass cruiser burn to the waterline in what seemed like three minutes because the captain didn't bother to ventilate the bilges after a lunch stop.

So I started at the bow and checked the hatches, the anchor locker, and all the compartments below the deck. When I got through with this, I thought how easy it would have been to wire an explosive to any one of the hatches I'd been flinging open so gaily. I checked the consoles and the seats, hung upside down to check the wiring and the controls, nothing new, no bright copper showing where a new connection had been made.

The steering steered and the throttles throttled and the gears seemed to engage. The lights worked and the horn. I went to check the rearmost hatch, the one just forward of the engines that you had to pry open with a screwdriver, and found it.

Some nice person had nicked the gas lines with an ice-pick, I suspect, a tiny pinhole on the bottom side of the fuel lines that you couldn't see. I never would have found it if I had not absently squeezed the black rubber balls that start the siphon process and put pressure in the lines. Under pressure, I got a gas drip, tiny but enough. The drip would continue as long as the engines were running and sucking fuel under pressure. Enough drops collect in the closed bilge and all you need is a spark.

Which he had arranged also.

The electric bilge pump sits in the lowest part of the bilge, far back and almost unreachable in the Grady-White. The insulation on the two wires had been stripped back a bit and the wires twisted together so that bare copper gleamed at bare copper about an eighth of an inch apart.

As a matter of habit, I run that pump offshore every hour or so. I would have perhaps half a gallon of gas and gasoline fumes in the bilges when I switched on the pump, causing a nice fat spark, if I followed my normal procedures. The accident would have been maybe half a dozen miles offshore, not an easy swim for a burned man.

Several mosquitoes came to dinner while I contemplated this.

Finally, I wrapped the wires after rerouting them properly and found some plastic-based tape that would fix the fuel lines. Then I pumped until my forearms hurt on the rubber balls to pressurize the system and hung upside down in the opening with a good light to make sure I had no further drip. I wiped up the few drops that had spilled, poured a couple of buckets of slipwater in the bilges and pumped it out with a manual pump I kept on board, and left the hatches up to let everything air out. In fifteen minutes I put on a life jacket and gingerly prepared to start up.

The youngest kid of the family who kept the bait camp, a

terminal smart-ass, complimented me on my good judgment on this, "since the weather's really building up here
in the slip." He laughed like a hyena at his wit. Nevertheless, I waited until he was inside his house before firing up.

And it ran like showroom new and I took it out in the
bay and used everything on board, pumps and radios and
depth finders and Loran, every gizmo and gadget I had,
until I was convinced there were no more surprises.

"Be a helluva fire, I betcha," I said aloud, heading back
in. I needed steak, bourbon, and a naked Kandy, in that
order.

Maybe I'd reverse the order.

27

THE PROBLEM IS, she hasn't done anything illegal. Questionable, maybe, discounting your story a trifle," said Hector Edfelter over the phone. I had made it a telephone consultation because every time I walked into his office I got popped for $125 for a "session." He had not as yet got to the point of charging for telephone conversations and I hoped fervently that he wouldn't compare notes with my lawyer, who did.

"Why the fuck do you have to discount my story?"

"Hearsay, hypothetical, circumstantial."

"She did fill me with weird drugs, she did make threats, she did take Kandy against her will, and she did try to blow me up. *After* she poisoned Vince's customers and girls."

"Even I, who know you, have difficulty with some of this. It just doesn't make sense. Why the vendetta? The logistics alone . . . And who's Kandy? You mean Tammy, right?"

So I had to explain and give a progress report (also hearsay) about Tammy's problem and what seemed to be the solution, which consisted mainly of her getting out of my clutches. Hector pointed out I always ended up with women whose names ended in "y" and I wondered if this was significant. He also said something about the zinc compounds and I remembered Melissa had said the same thing. Better living through chemistry.

My frustration had reached meltdown.

"What in the screaming fuck am I supposed to do!"

"Beaumont," he said, annoyed. "You're talking about a doctor, a scientist, with a national reputation. She's been asked to speak at several national meetings this year. One I'm going to in a couple weeks conflicts with a national convention and they asked her to give a *taped* speech. That's fairly strong, right?"

"Her colleagues love and respect her. But she does weird shit and scams the insurance."

"People who are emotionally involved sometimes get their perceptions warped. Especially if the other person 'dumped' them. Normal setbacks and accidents become part of the plot. 'They' assume supernormal powers. Evil lurks in the hearts of men. Women too."

"I'm the dumper, not the dumpee!"

"Nonetheless, I'm sure there's a reasonable explanation for all this. Why am I giving you all this shrinky advice for free? Maybe you need to come in?"

"No, thanks. You explain the 'reasonableness' to my buddy Vince, okay? And just what am I supposed to do, struggling here with my warped perceptions?"

"Take two aspirin and call me in the morning?"

My shrink refused to take me seriously. It shook me. Maybe the whole thing was a paranoid fantasy? Hector excused his joke and said, "I'll speak to her again. She's giving a paper at the APA regional meeting too."

"Hector. Please be discreet. The last time you spoke to her, she whacked me with weird stuff."

"That's me, discreet. Anyhow it's six months off." And he told me a bad joke about an elephant and a mouse. Should therapists tell dirty jokes?

The worst part about the whole lashup was that there was no path toward a solution. Perhaps it was her shrink insights, the knowledge that uncertainty is the worst trauma of all, that anything can be endured if you can see a way out. But I wasn't 100 percent sure that there was a vendetta going, much less knowing a way to resolve it. It could have been a normal wear-and-tear gas leak and I could have wired the bilge pump so that vibration wore off the insulation and Kandy could have caught a drink just the wrong way; Vince's place could be food poisoning: it's possible.

But she was a woman, albeit a strange and remarkable woman. This meant, in my mind, that she was more matter-of-fact savage than I could dream of being. Practical too. She had a ton of money at her disposal, the power of the magic M.D. behind her name, a happy cohort in Nelson. And I knew damn well that I had slugged and drugged Dr. Natelson, role reversal, to get out of the clinic, and nobody screamed for cops or filed lawsuits.

So in the end I decided to trust my judgment rather than Hector's skepticism. I called him back to get the particulars on his shrink meeting two weeks hence where her taped speech would be her stand-in. You can edit tape.

"You're not planning some sort of scene?"

"Hector. This is Beaumont."

"Answer the question."

"Not me. Although you're totally wrong about the bitch."

"You really should come in and let's talk this out."

"Give me the details, Hector. I have the Polaroids."

And in the end he did, with many warnings, cautions, admonitions. And I had to promise to come in and talk the whole thing over. But I had a date, a time, and a place.

Even the rudiments of a plan.

"Look," I said into the phone, sincere voice, overtones of worry. "This is getting to be a drag. For both of us. Let's just have a truce, you go your way and I'll do my thing. And no more, we're even, Kings-X, enough."

"This means you will abandon your efforts for my competition, dear Beaumont? And come back to me?"

"Melissa, you're asking me to give up a chunk of billing. Plus a lot of fun, in the professional sense."

"Nevertheless, these are my conditions."

"I'll resign the hospital account. But also I won't do your stuff. I assume that's what you mean."

"I mean business and personal."

"I didn't know you cared." I sneered.

"Does this mean yes?"

"I'll give up the business. But I'm afraid that's all."

"And I'm afraid that's not enough. I want you where I can con—have you. In all senses of the word."

She laughed. Melissa had a horrible laugh. This one went on a couple of seconds too long. I had a quick vision of glittering, feral eyes.

"Come on, Melissa," I interrupted. "Enough's enough, okay?"

"You heard me," she said. "What next, you wonder?"

More laughter. I hung up but I did say good-bye.

I had always recorded Dr. Stone's radio spots at the same studio. The first couple of times she had gone with me to observe, me playing the ad-biggie to the hilt. You can go to the radio stations and get the stuff done for nearly free, but the sound quality was better at the private studios as was the engineering talent. Most of the studios had all sorts of fascinating equipment that you never used but it gave you a low-cost way to feel high tech. By comparison to the television production houses, which *were* high tech and you paid for it through the nose.

If she was gonna do a taped speech, it was a good bet she'd go to these folks for the recording, seeking expert editing, even background music for all I know. I booked myself a block of time, wrote some scripts for several clients, and arranged to meet the announcers there. I made it late afternoon and specified the engineer I wanted, a man who barely managed to hold his job, due to certain essential weaknesses. Old Crow and anything female.

"Kandy," I said. "Just how adroit are you?"

"Adroit?"

"In your dubious profession, you tend to hold out a rather obvious carrot, right?"

"And the sticks we don't need to talk about."

"Correct, smart-ass. My question is: Can you tantalize, dazzle, confuse, and lead on a horny man? Enough so he forgets what he's doing and leaves me alone in his studio?"

"Child's play."

"Although you remain . . . essentially untouched."

"No sacrifice?"

"What I'm afraid of, my dear, is that you might not find it a sacrifice."

"Don't worry, Beaumont. For an old guy, you got good moves." And she kissed me with considerable enthusiasm and I explained what it was I wanted her to do.

We had two weeks. I called Dr. Stone and begged for time to consider her proposition. She was insistent, pointing out that I could ruin her plans with "unfounded accusations," which I pointed out were rather founded. She asked who they'd believe and reminded me of the court records. I sounded like I was weakening and Kandy made disgusted faces all over the place and finally poured an entire bucket of ice from the fridge down my shorts.

It may have helped the impression of controlled terror I was trying to achieve. In any event, Dr. Stone graciously agreed finally, made a salacious remark I didn't believe, laughing immoderately again, and I got off the phone.

If this was going to work out, I'd need a good second-story man. I called Vince and made my request. I believe in giving suppliers a reasonable amount of lead time.

And we needed a good cat burglar. The papers were currently full of a well-meaning lady who had arranged for the murder of her lover's wife, using her own credit cards to rent the car and motel room for the hired killer. She had some difficulty explaining the signed receipts and was currently locked up for an extended vacation.

Any explanations I had to make, praise god it wouldn't occur, had to be reasonable.

28

I RECORDED SOME VERY nice radio spots, one or two of which I might actually use. Kandy had outdone herself, making her thirty years appear an especially ripe twenty-four or so, complete with tennies and white socks. No bra and Hank the Engineer could barely push his buttons and twist his knobs for staring. One of my announcers, a rather emphatically gay guy who was skinny and wearing a toga-type outfit, finally got annoyed at the repeated technical errors and came in and set the dials himself.

"Just don't fuck with these, okay?" he said in his basso profundo voice. Then he went back and cut two spots (voice of doom for cocaine addicts) in one take each and flounced out, advising me to try a rival studio next time.

When we got through, Kandy got the grand tour at

Hank's suggestion and I was left in the control room. I love it when the plot works. I was into the master reels before the double doors had shut behind the two of them.

The masters were kept on half-inch tape, metal reels, and they had a very precise filing system, kept by date. It took me about four minutes to figure out which reel was "Stone, Convention Speech." I made myself a dub onto plain old quarter-inch stock I had brought in my briefcase and tested it to make sure I had set the board properly.

It was déjà vu, in a sense. I had done something similar once before and survived. But everything was in order and I was looking bored when they came back. Hank's hands were hovering and you could almost see him itch, but Kandy stuck out her hand to shake and we were out of there.

"It's a joke, right?" My DJ friend with the home recording studio was a touch nervous. I had laboriously transcribed the speech and then made some alterations in the copy. He had a four-track machine on which we could assemble a Beaumont version of Dr. Stone's speech with some significant changes. He did a final checkout of the equipment, made sure I knew how to work everything and left, after repeated reassurances.

My version was a dilly and I got enthused as I worked the board. *The federally sponsored as well as the private insurance plans make it possible for the mental health care industry to deliver a standard of care unmatched in the world* became, in my version, *The federally sponsored as well as the private insurance plans make it possible for the mental health care industry to achieve significant, even windfall, profits,* for example.

Patients who do not need hospitalization but who can benefit from outpatient group became *Patients who do not need to be hospitalized but we can benefit if they are.* So forth.

The writing task was a bit of a challenge since I had to use words that existed in the original speech, dubbing and overdubbing to get everything in the right place. Then, since people end sentences with a down inflection, we had to manipulate the pitch of her voice with a variable speed control. My buddy had a gadget called a Lexicon that allowed him to compress or lengthen the pauses between words, which helped a bunch. But there remained a ton of splicing and editing and I had to double the already-exorbitant fee to get him to finish.

In the end, we had a true version of Dr. Stone's philosophy on tape. We also had a very nervous DJ friend, who made me swear great oaths that I would never tell where the speech came from or who had done the editing. I even had to use my own boxes and reels so as to leave no way to trace it back to him.

I left after several more promises as he was busy destroying our work tapes. I thought he could simply erase them, but he was adamant. Probably would wipe all fingerprints clean too.

Kandy was alternately aghast and delighted when I played my version for her. Dr. Stone agreed that patients were a slimy lot who mainly deserved to be taken. Dr. Stone advised her colleagues to routinely pad their charges since the insurance companies paid "usual and customary" fees. If they all raised prices, the payments would go up. Dr. Stone described the woman's movement as ripe for the picking and advocated free and open sexuality between patients and therapists. There was plenty more.

In my version, Dr. Stone *said* what Dr. Stone *did*, and that may be the biggest no-no there is in our hypocritical culture. The end result would be described as provocative and disturbing in the lay press. And Lord help her when her jealous peers got a hold of her. I worried about the transcript that would be handed out at the meeting after the tape but decided trying to fake one and get it distributed was beyond my abilities. Hell, they'd believe their ears, rather than a transcript. And they could always run the tape again.

What I had, of course, did me no good, unless I could switch it with Dr. Stone's copy of the original. The speech was about fourteen minutes (a bit too long in my professional judgment since she had no visuals to hold the audience) and it would have routinely been put on a five-inch reel. The reel would be in a standard box.

I called Vince and asked if his guy was ready for B&E. He was offended that I asked and said, "Naturally."

"He understands he's doing a switch and he can't touch anything else?"

"Naturally."

"And he won't give in to temptation?"

"Beaumont," he said, offended even more. "She's a pro and I hired her. Don't worry. Where will the tape be?"

"Vince," I said, "I'm glad to see you're an equal opportunity aider and abetter. Melissa probably will keep the tape at the hospital until she sends it off. The meeting's next Friday, so it should be on its way soon. You want to make the switch after the convention's started when nobody will listen to it to check. Say in the wee hours Friday morning."

"You did get the hotel and the room right?"

"Vince!" I said, offended in turn.

"Okay, okay. One more thing . . . send the cash now."

"You've been talking to your girls again, Vince," I said. "The cash is on its way."

A couple more phone calls describing a provocative, even shocking address to be given at the meeting to the medical writers at both papers and to a crusading TV lady who wanted to out-consumer-advocate the world finished my tasks.

I thought about giving my ex-friend fair warning but decided the hell with it. Her weird laugh echoed in my mind.

29

K<small>ANDY</small>," I <small>SAID</small> as I stacked up the last of my insertion orders, "I've decided that you need a new career."

"What's wrong with shaking my ass at the geeks?"

"It's unseemly and my mother wouldn't approve and you don't learn the proper respect for money when guys stuff it in your pants. Have you ever reflected on the symbolism involved?"

"Beaumont, you're a stuffy ol' geek yourself. You never seemed to mind when we weren't together. And, in point of fact, I seem to recall some rather admiring glances—stares actually—back at Vince's when Suki and Melanie were doing their lesbian number."

It was a lazy Saturday afternoon and I had decided to change the course of my love's life now that the insertion orders were finished. We would have a good month next month, thanks to the new hospital. Never say that mental health isn't a paying proposition. And the ads were dynamite. I preened a bit, mentally.

"That's a touch different. Any red-blooded American boy would be interested in such perversions. Besides I was watching the choreography."

"All four of them."

"Really. Anyway, why don't you come work for me?"

"Doing what?"

"Production art. What design we need. An illustration now and again. Put into practice what you've learned in school."

"And I get to sleep with the boss, right?"

"Fringes. We call them fringes."

"Beaumont," she said, coming over to kiss my nose. "You've got an asset, your glib tongue. And you use it to make money on those rare occasions when you decide to work at it. I've got some assets and I'm using them. The fact that it offends your sense of puritan possessiveness is not my problem."

"Who said it was a problem?" I said weakly.

"Why don't you come watch me work?"

"Two thousand a month, I think we can afford that."

"Would I earn it? And you haven't answered my question."

She was dead serious and I had to stop and try to get in touch with my feelings. Here, Feelings, nice, Feelings, where are you, you little sunbitches!

"Okay," I said. "I give a bit on the possessiveness. I know it's bad and rotten and inhuman and all but I just don't like you using—showing—your bod for money."

"Using my brain is okay?" she said dangerously. "How 'bout if I was a telephone lineperson and climbed poles?"

"It's the sexual aspect. Isn't it a bit tawdry?"

"It's sad is what it is," she said slowly. "Sad because the

bulk of these guys haven't the slightest idea of how to go about having a real relationship with a woman so they come to clubs. The relationship is safe because they pay for it here."

"The world's oldest profession, part two?"

"Something like that. They can understand the rules. And all they have to put up is a few bucks."

"But you don't have to be involved in this sad business, do you?"

"Ol' buddy, when you show me how to clear twenty-five hundred or more a month for thirty hours worth of work each week, you'll be talking my language."

"Pretty please? With sugar on it?"

"I'm only good for a couple or three more years. You can stand it that long. Do you realize I'll be thirty next month?"

"I still wish—"

"Beaumont. It turns me on, a little, to boot. Ask your shrink. Have you heard anything about *the* shrink?"

"The meeting was last night. I haven't heard any atomic explosions from the direction of Houston and Vince hasn't called to report his girl got arrested. So I don't know."

"*That's* a respectable profession for a lady. Second-story Beach Blanket Bikini Party! We going offshore in the A of M?"

"Let's catch the weather tonight and decide. I'll go chase up some mullet, just in case."

Which is exactly what I did, stalking the shiny little critters on my favorite oyster reef, tossing the eight-foot-diameter castnet in front of them as they fled my footsteps on the crunchy shell.

It is not terribly rewarding to be a mullet.

When I had a couple of dozen captured and in the bait well, I turned on the aerator to help them stay alive during the night. The aerator, which is nothing more than a bilge pump rigged to pick up water from the well and spray it

out, thereby acquiring oxygen, reminded me of my previous troubles, and I checked the boat out stem to stern
and found everything working, which is unusual with
boats.

If we didn't go out in the morning, I'd turn the mullet
loose and they'd have a wonderful mullet story to tell their
grandchildren. All seven million of them.

Kandy was struggling with her famous fried chicken
when I got back to the house just before dark. It is truly a
work of art although she is not dish-efficient. I usually
scrubbed the pots and pans without complaint, assuming I
hadn't eaten so much I had to let them wait till I'd recovered on the couch.

Tonight I managed to stay just this side of comatose from
overeating, issued my effusive compliments to the chef, and
manfully cleaned acres of dirty implements.

Then we retired to the couch and I fiddled with the TV,
channel 13 from Houston, with a round-faced anchorman
who must have been the best adjusted person on earth because he was always pleasant and happy, even when reporting hurricanes and multicar pileups and an epidemic of
assaults on the elderly.

"They can't run very fast," Kandy said darkly as this last
item came up and I hushed her to watch the weather. One-
to three-foot swells, piece of cake, high tide at 3 A.M. and a
strong low at ten in the morning.

What more could a boy want?

"A final item," said the anchor with a small grin as the
weather ended. "A major brouhaha is brewing tonight in
psychology circles after a nationally known figure in the
field gave a tape-recorded speech in which she claimed the
major motivation of the mental health professional should
be monetary gain. She also allegedly stated that it was perfectly proper for psychologists and psychiatrists to have sex
with their patients . . . of either sex. Dr. Melissa Stone
of . . ."

"Oh, shit," said Kandy.

"Shush," I said.

The reporting was fair and accurate, I thought, given my knowledge of the contents of the speech. I wished he had brought up the bit about the feminists being easy pickings for unscrupulous shrinks but maybe that would be covered in the morning when our anchorperson promised a follow-up story and a taped interview with Dr. Stone. Who was denying the whole thing, it seemed.

I avoided Kandy's eyes and there was a silence.

"Well, she started it—" I began.

Kandy ignored me, her body tense. "Beaumont, there's somebody outside," she said in a whisper.

30

I LEAPED LIKE A MADMAN to douse the lights and joined Kandy at the window to peer down at the interloper. I didn't recognize the car and I would have been relieved to see a pickup, since everybody I knew on the coast drove them. The figure behind the wheel was fussing with something, vaguely outlined against the mercury vapor light a hundred yards away. No wind, I noticed. Fishing would be good tomorrow.

"He's not very big," Kandy said dubiously as the person got out of the car, interior lights going on, but we couldn't see much due to the angle.

"That's because he's a she," I said, catching a flash of blonde hair.

"Oh, God, it's Dr. Stone and she's going to shotgun us!"

"No shotgun," I said. "Oh, shit."

"What?"

"I know her," I said, going to the door. Then I went outside and walked halfway down the steps to greet Tammy. All girls' names end in "y." Did Miss Manners have a prescription for this situation? Was my zipper zipped? God help me if they ganged up on me. Guilt washed over me.

"Hey, babe," I said bravely, "long time et cetera."

She didn't say anything, just grinned at me and wrapped me up in a hug. I tried to do a friend hug, bent over from the waist to keep our nether regions apart, but she was having none of this and pressed against me top to bottom. She was crying a little.

Felt pretty much like the old Tammy too, near as I could remember. At least there were definite bumps and curves, very female, and I suspected Kandy was sharpening the fillet knife upstairs prior to castration. Maybe she'd be dulling it, and I extricated myself and said, "Damn, you look good. It's great to see you!"

"Beaumont," she said, "you asshole."

Got 'em wrapped around my finger, that's me, I thought.

"You're in big trouble and they kicked me out of Group. I weigh one sixteen!"

"Way to go! Come upstairs and . . . ah . . . meet . . . there's somebody you need to . . . I've . . ."

"And in the on-deck circle it's . . ." she said in an announcer's voice.

"Kandy," I said, and led her upstairs.

I suspect that the Victorian manners we studied in high school were invented to keep folks from running swords through one another at regular intervals. Perhaps this is the root of all manners. In any event, our social mores have not caught up with our social customs.

I was what you call your basic ill at ease.

The ladies were arching their metaphorical pinkies away

from imaginary cups of tea and exchanging pleasantries in icy voices. Everything I tried fell flat: my "Glad you're up and about" being followed quickly by Kandy's comment: "We heard you were flat on your back," an obvious untruth, which Tammy returned by asking something about hundred-dollar tips.

"Oh, shit," I said finally, "let's get drunk."

"I don't drink anymore," said Tammy, which didn't do a whole lot for the atmosphere but then she pulled a joint out of her purse, lighted same and passed it to Kandy. Hell, I took a hit myself, mostly antidrug these days but this was an extreme circumstance. By the time the joint was down to fingertip-burning stage, we were all in a better mood.

"Ouch," said Kandy, burning her fingers. "'Just say no.'"

"No," Tammy and I said simultaneously, and we all laughed immoderately.

"So why am I in big trouble?" I asked.

"Because Dr. Stone is on the warpath and the lights are burning brightly at all clinics. And the ships at sea," Tammy added.

"We heard the TV newscast," Kandy said.

"I heard what she said, that speech, on the talk station, the one that you can get all over? Why would she say that?"

"Because it's there," I said.

"Because Beaumont bolixed-up her tape," Kandy said.

"Everything I did was the truth!"

"And the truth shall set Dr. Stone on the warpath. Boy, is she pissed," said Tammy. "Henry told me I had to leave Group, and the way he did it made it sound like she'd cut my head off."

"Who is Henry?"

"Dr. Natelson."

"Little Hitler?" I was amazed. I didn't think this would

be the person Tammy was interested in. I felt a faint stirring of jealous unease, surely she had better taste.

"I think it's cute!" Tammy said indignantly. "How does it feel to take your clothes off in public? If that's not too personal." I started to protest that I removed my clothes in the privacy of my own home or at the YMCA and realized she had addressed Kandy.

"It's just a phase—"

Kandy interrupted me. "It's arrogant to answer questions directed at me, asshole. It's a power trip and then it gets boring and it does not give one a good opinion of the male sex or the general level of the population's intelligence, if you want to know the truth," she replied to Tammy.

"Do you know?" I asked the room. "That both of you have called me 'asshole' in the last half hour?"

"Take it as a hint," Kandy said, and Tammy laughed like a bastard. "It's a little bit sexy, sometimes," she said to Tammy, who looked thoughtful.

"I lack the confidence."

"You'd be great!" Kandy reassured her. "Fresh and sweet and that all-American look . . . they'd eat it up."

"No recruitment, please," I murmured.

"Beaumont, you asshole," they said together.

I floated away a little, miffed that my conversational efforts were being universally rejected. I wondered about the little mullet in the bait well. Then I went out on the deck to look at the moon, only to find there was none. I wondered what happened to the moon. Inside the ladies were in an animated discussion, seemingly friendly, and I thought that was nice. I wanted an Oreo badly.

"Does anybody want a peanut butter and jelly sandwich?" I asked, sticking my head in the door, and that inspired Kandy to bring out the rest of the fried chicken and we had a picnic without ants. I claimed full credit for this. Also Oreos and milk, nothing ever tasted better.

"I'll just sit here and have quiet sexual fantasies about the two of you," I announced when we were through.

"Only an asshole would assume we were interested," said Tammy. "Don't you like the way I assert myself?"

"Not particularly," I said.

"Very much," said Kandy.

"I was not implying anything," I protested. "Nor assuming anything. I'll watch my mind carefully."

"First you'll have to find it," said Kandy, and they thought this was especially witty.

Then they resumed their conversation and I meditated. "Wax," said Kandy, "I have to wax all the time. Because you're blonde, you'd probably not be bothered so much."

"You're blonde too."

"I have to help it along."

"Deception," I said. "Cosmetics in general are deception."

I received twin glances of appraisal tinged with disgust and waved my hands in surrender. "Just thinking out loud."

"Have you ever noticed how they're so quick to criticize us and how much fussing they do when they think it counts?" asked Tammy.

"My god! The shirts aren't on hangers!" Kandy mimicked a man's voice. Their eyes glittered.

"Have you been using my razor again!" screamed Tammy in her best attempt at a gruff male voice.

"Goddamn it! Where are my cufflinks!"

"Am I losing any hair in back?" Tammy whimpered.

"*I* don't need to ask directions, *I* can read a map," Kandy responded.

"What's all this funny sauce on the meat?" Tammy made an elaborate pantomime of a cautious eater.

"Boy! I bet that's the best you've ever had! Snore," said Kandy, puffing out her chest.

"I love it when you moan like that." Tammy laughed.

"It *is* in!" screamed Kandy, and they both rolled around on the floor in helpless laughter. I had never said or even thought about saying any of the above and I told them so in a cold voice.

Somehow my thoughts of a ménage à trois, even if I were having them, seemed inappropriate and I wondered aloud what Dr. Stone would do.

"I have no idea what she will do, but there's a lady who *might* do anything. I've heard a lot of funny stuff about some of her groups," said Tammy.

"I think they're mostly legal gang-bangs."

"There are precedents for nonstressful sexual encounters in a permissive therapeutic atmosphere," Kandy said theatrically. "And clinical proof that this can be helpful in some cases of dysfunction."

"Sexual dysfunction," added Tammy for my benefit.

"I didn't know you were an expert," I said to Kandy.

"You haven't been watching, Jack," she replied, and winked at Tammy, who giggled.

It is most disquieting to have your previous lover and your current lover in the same room, winking and giggling.

"I wonder if we might ought to buy us a motel room or two over to Port Lavaca," I mused. "Just in case."

Then we heard the car doors slamming outside. It was far too late for visiting. Amazing how quickly I got straight. Both ladies were rigid and quiet, looking at me. Did they think I knew something, maybe spinach on my teeth? Point Lookout, even on the weekends, averages about one car an hour. After 10 P.M., nobody came visiting unless there was a death.

I hoped that this would prove an exception.

31

It was a cliché Mercedes, that much I could see in the cold blue mercury vapor light. It was parked behind Tammy's car, crosswise. Apparently whoever wasn't too concerned about Tammy getting the car out. Somehow I suspected Tammy would like to get the car out, no matter how much fun we had been having Beaumont-baiting. Tammy had my left arm in a tight grip while Kandy was crawling on my right shoulder. I wanted to ask them why they thought I could offer protection.

None of us was making jokes all of a sudden.

The problem with my house was that the outside staircase was the only way in or out, unless we felt like ripping open a window, removing a screen, and leaping fourteen feet.

Two people got out of the car and started up the stairs

and I went out to meet them. They were dressed for the bay, sort of, shorts and shirts and socks with boat shoes.

"Melissa, what a surprise. Not necessarily a *nice* surprise but a surprise. Aren't you supposed to be doing a TV interview?"

Jesus, I felt like a Ping-Pong ball. This back-and-forth shit had to come to an end. Who would she capture and drug next, Bullit? I was proud of my tone and delivery. I couldn't see who the guy was until they were almost at the top and then it was my second least favorite shrink, Natelson.

"Jesus Christ," I said. "Get me some crazy people, quick! We got the first team here."

I didn't move and the advantage of being higher should have given me the upper hand. Plus it was my house. But Melissa showed me a handgun, which tended to obliterate the more subtle psychological advantages. Girl had changed her style. No more chemical punishments, just a crude, flat black hand weapon capable of punching large holes in people, yuck. She held it like she knew it well.

Her voice was flat, mechanical. No curious up inflections. Dead sounding. "Move and go inside," she said, and waved the gun. I shrugged and obeyed.

The ladies were holding hands and Natelson was visibly surprised to see Tammy. "I told you . . ." he began, and dropped it.

"How's the jaw, Doc?" I asked, and he hit me with a nonprofessional look. I was one up on the physical level and always would be but he looked like he was going to change venues and try for a rematch.

"Surely you can recognize the reality we have here."

"Tell me about it. Thirty-two-caliber reality, I take it. Oh, Kandy, this is Dr. Stone. I've told you about her and I think she's your druggist. And this is Dr. Natelson, one of her happy colleagues. You-all know Tammy, of course, Dr.

Natelson especially. And I'm the poor dummy who owns the joint. What do you want?"

"A retraction/confession, of course," Natelson said. I was bothered by the fact that he was the spokesperson and that he was nervous. "Clear vindication of Dr. Stone, reparations for the damages done her professional reputation, a concise explanation of how you manipulated the tape." Why did they care? Want a technical explanation of tape-splicing and creative use of the editor? Melissa spoke up finally, flatly.

"That is the minor part. It is unfortunate you have these people here." She lighted a Winston and looked for an ashtray. I pointed at the coffee table, the perfect host.

"Tammy, I want you to leave at once," Natelson said, forgetting about his lousy parking job.

"No one may leave," Melissa stated without looking at him.

"Is this gun therapy, Dr. Stone?" I suffer from terminal smart-ass. But goddamn it, it was my house and I was more sinned against than sinning. "The Use of the Thirty-Two Caliber in Field Experiments?"

Natelson shot me an acid, can't-you-see glare and tried to soothe things. He looked as frightened as I should, oddly. "The gun is merely to ensure that there will be no violence, Mr. Beaumont."

"Fuckin' for chastity, fightin' for peace?"

"I have no need of repartee," Melissa said. I didn't like the way she talked or the pinpoint pupils or the unwavering hand. Guns are nasty things. They do focus your attention wonderfully well, I observed.

"Melissa," I started in my best public relations counselor voice. "As your one-time publicity advisor, I've got to tell you that the best thing to do is dismiss the whole thing. Obviously, you have been had. You only draw attention to it by fussing. You might also get off my back generally, since you seem to be much better at dishing it out than taking it."

"Mr. Beaumont!" Natelson began, and I interrupted.

"Ladies! You haven't said a word! Don't you agree we were having a *much* better time before our guests arrived? Maybe they'll take the hint. I hope so, don't you?"

Tammy appeared not to hear me. She was studying Natelson like she had never seen a male before. Strange creature this. Walks and talks. Who would have thought I'd actually see one?

Kandy was hovering protectively close to her and her expression said she wished for a large-enough slipper to squash these bugs that had scuttled out from a previously unknown crevice. Also fear and repugnance. Cockroach looks.

I felt I held repartee honors so I could quit.

"Disclaimers and confessions and explanations are bullshit, Melissa," I said quietly. "Makes you look worse, actually, best to just move on and grin at it."

"You will do as I say," she replied in her mechanical voice. Sounded like a cancer patient with his throat mike box. Can a cigarette voice just start suddenly?

"Jokes over, visiting hours are through," I said briskly. "Let's move 'em out, folks, I'm tired and I want to go to bed."

Dr. Natelson was visibly annoyed. "You must take this seriously," he said. "You have placed in jeopardy something that took me a number of years to arrange and that generates more bottomline money than you can possibly comprehend."

"Whoa. You arranged this deal? The scam with the Alphabet Units? I thought Dr. Stone here was the Big Guy."

"The concept was mine," he said proudly. What a creep. "Melissa came along and expanded it, served as an excellent . . . symbol, scholarly symbol, for our work. She has also added a great deal, handled insurance reviews and the like, made it operate perfectly. The logistics alone . . ."

Tammy looked horrified. Another idol cracked, shit. The

sonuvabitch shouldn't screw around with patients, much less poor patients who believed he was governed by psychological ethics and ideals. This bastard needed to be running a Greek multinational, arming Third World countries and starving babies. He had done her some good, weight wise, though, give the devil his due.

"So you're the big cheese? I'll be damned."

"Yes," he said semiproudly.

"No," Melissa said. "It no longer matters." He looked at her in horror. Prestige and pecking order mattered a lot to old Dr. Natelson. I thought we should focus on the situation at hand, Melissa's hand, the one with the gun. Live in the Now, Dr. N.

"And who decided to shoot me full of happy juice?" I asked.

"Which time?" Natelson said. "Oh, I suppose it was a joint decision, right, Dr. Stone?"

"But you're my *doctor*," Tammy wailed.

"This is outside the therapeutic situation," he said uncomfortably. "And it has nothing to do with . . . with whatever personal . . . with anything."

"You made him, it's your fault, you're doing this to him," she screamed at Melissa.

"Too much aimless talk," Melissa said remotely. "There is no one around to come to your rescue, Beaumont." Still no variation in tone, this-is-a-recording. "You will recall, you explained how isolated this place is."

Bullit growled from her corner, distracting us all. For a small dog, she has definite opinions, and I believe she had taken a dislike to Dr. Stone. She began to advance, stiff-legged and fluffed up, and Kandy scooped her up as Melissa moved the gun toward the floor.

"Well, that settles that," I said brightly. "Even the dog wants you to leave." Bullit would make me pay later for the "even." I was wishing real hard for Mr. Evans to run out of bourbon and come borrow a cup. I would have wel-

comed little green men from Mars or an earthquake, although we run few earthquakes to the century in Texas.

"There's no need for threats, implicit or otherwise," said Natelson. His voice had the uncertain bluster of an insecure substitute teacher facing the seniors. Had I but known the real relationship, the good doctor and his star protégée, I could have gone to the source and probably saved everybody a lot of agony. Natelson seemed like someone a man could reason with. Or beat up, at least. What Melissa was currently was anybody's guess, although given a safe viewing chamber, I suspect she'd make an interesting case history. Natelson went on, casting a nervous eye toward his partner. "Merely write and sign a statement and we'll be off. Any further legal action—"

"We are not leaving until punishment," said Melissa. Oh, shit. Avenging angels I could do without. Binding arbitration maybe?

"Melissa, we discussed this and came to a consensus," Natelson said sharply, turning to face her. "I do not wish to be a party to violence in any form."

"Punishment," she said simply. You could see in his face that he realized things were seriously amiss.

He continued onward in his board room voice. "The confession is punishment enough. Later we can discuss whatever financial reparations—"

"Enough," she said, and the gun swung in his direction. I admired the way he slipped into his professional stance without a pause. Unfortunately, you could see him reminding himself to show no fear and act decisively.

"Perhaps it would be better if I held the gun for a time," he said soothingly. "Just for a few moments, until we have reached an agreement in principle." And he advanced a cautious step, hand out. She extended the gun, bracing her right hand with her left.

"Jeez, just like TV," Kandy said sarcastically, and I loved her for it. Her voice did not waver. I didn't want to try mine.

"Fuck it," said Tammy, mostly to herself. "I always screw the wrong guys."

Natelson and Melissa seemed stuck in the pose. He wheedled and she pointed guns. "Now, you will recall that we have agreed that this was the best course of action, after considerable discussion," he said reasonably. "I will not and cannot permit violence. Give the gun to me!" He started toward her.

She shot him squarely in the chest.

One of the most desirable attributes an Ad Biggie like I once wanted to be can have is an eclectic knowledge of virtually everything. Some might claim a smattering of knowledge about weird subjects is hardly an indication of scholarship or even intelligence, but it comes in handy writing ad copy.

To this end, I read continually. I occasionally picked up a survivalist magazine or *Soldier of Fortune* to try to get some indication of the elements of that mindset. These folks tended to sneer at the thirty-two caliber for its lack of knockdown power and quote bullet weights and velocity, footpounds of energy at the muzzle and so forth.

Dr. Natelson probably wouldn't agree.

A spray of bright-red blood splashed against the wall behind him. That meant arterial, I think. His body reacted as if I had taken a full swing with a baseball bat and whacked him in the chest, and he was flung back and to the side. A sharp odor came from him, mingling with the arid smell of gunpowder, I suppose. His pants stained at the crotch.

Bullit was going crazy in Kandy's arms and Tammy was screaming without making a sound, tendons in the neck stretched tight and visible.

Melissa swung back toward me and said, "Punishment."

Natelson flopped a bit on the floor and was still.

32

I HAVE NEVER FELT quite so alone.

The expert at dealing with crazy persons was on the floor and I thought he was dead and the crazy person (we were well past the need for euphemisms) was there to be dealt with. If I thought one of the ladies could have handled her, I would have gladly crawled back in the corner and watched. But Melissa was focused on me and my friends were immobilized by shock and somebody had to do something and guess who owned the black bean?

"I can see we'll have to do what you say," I said quietly.

"Of course."

"Right now, I suppose the situation can be handled," I continued conversationally. "How do you plan to keep it that way?"

"Punishment."

"I understand punishment but you *do* want to avoid any
further publicity problems, contact with the police, that sort
of thing." I looked for agreement and got a tiny nod.
I spread my hands in inquiry.
"Perhaps if you let these two go . . ."
"That would be quite stupid," Melissa said in a reasonable tone. "They would immediately cause trouble."
"You don't feel they could be trusted to remain silent,
knowing that your . . . wrath . . . and also that they need
your counseling, therapy?"
"Don't treat me like a fool! Punishment!"
"What, then?" I really wanted to understand her crazy
logic.
"It was an accident, obviously. The authorities need to
see that, I have many pressing engagements, cannot be
bothered by . . . it was clearly an accident, unfortunate, but
the work must be continued, shielded . . ."
I wondered how many accidents included a bullet hole. I
suspect that most killers, in the first few minutes after the
irrevocable action is taken, seek the reassurance of accident, the disavowment of responsibility, I didn't really
mean . . .
"Certainly," I said. "It is . . . unfortunate. Now we must,
now we need damage control."
"You killed him," shrieked Tammy. Thanks a lot.
Melissa's eyes flicked to her and I could see the decision
being formed.
"Two accidents won't wash, Melissa!" I yelled.
"Quiet!" she said to Tammy. Kandy moved over and put
an arm around her and soothed her. Both of them were
crying a little. I felt like wetting my pants. Nobody was
looking at Natelson, who already had, and I thought of a
distraction.
"Suppose I check to see how badly Dr. Natelson is in-
jured, Dr. Stone," I said formally.
She nodded and I knelt beside him. I could smell him.

No pulse, no movement. I wasn't about to touch his chest, seeping red through the white shirt. His legs were nearly hairless and white in his tailored bush shorts. Skinny too.

"I think the shock may have been too much," I reported. "I can't seem to find a pulse." If she would just come to check him, I could get an opportunity and we'd have two docs on the floor. But she seemed indifferent.

"An accident," she repeated.

"Yeah, so we'd better call for an ambulance and the cops. The EMS people around here are really good, I did a brochure on them, response time is—"

"You do not seem able to comprehend simple English," she said irritated. "We will call no one. I'll . . . I'll file a report."

Maybe a paper. *The Journal of the American Psychiatric Association* will love it. Way to go, Melissa. Without asking permission, I went into the bedroom and ripped the cover off the bed and threw it over Natelson. I heard her say something but figured acting like I was free might get me to that happy state. One exit only, damn it.

I stood as far away from the ladies as possible. If she started shooting, maybe one or two of us could get away if we were scattered out. In a twenty- by twenty-four-foot area, only so much scattering is possible but I tried. I also tried to send Kandy a mental message but she continued to comfort Tammy. All girls' names end in "y." What would Hector do?

"Would you like something to drink? Smirnoff?"

"Nothing, thank you," Melissa said automatically, and I went to the kitchen area and began to mix myself one. I also splashed some bourbon over a couple of ice cubes in two glasses and took it to the girls. "Medicine," I said. "Drink it."

It was a strange cocktail party. I was trying to get Melissa used to the idea of me moving around. Thought I might have a chance with a thrown bourbon bottle, but she must have sensed my intent and moved close to Kandy with the gun pointed directly at her.

I didn't want a repeat, oh god, not Kandy stretched out on the floor, wet pants when the sphincter lets go, smell of blood and death. Not anybody, ever, let me out of this. And I had a sharp mental image of the gleaming point of a gaff penetrating the side of a fish and the writhing.

"Well, you can't afford any more people with bullet holes in them," I pointed out. "So I think you should put up the gun. If you agree," I added hastily, remembering Natelson.

She smiled. "The gun is the only reason you're obeying. You should obey me because I'm the Doctor." Also singsong. I was not tempted to sing along. "But I have the gun," she said.

"Well, perhaps. But you could put it up and we could all sit down and figure a way out of this," I said, pointing to the table.

"You sit down." And I did and she motioned the girls to join me. Then Melissa stood at the end of the table, gun now loose in her hand pointing at the floor, much like a teacher with her attentive pupils. Natelson was much less bothersome covered up.

"It's quite a lot of money," she said brightly, "but that's far from being my full motivation. You see, girls have it hard and I have it very hard, being responsible for so many others. They have to do as I say, you see, in order to get well. I like it when they get well? But there's the money, of course, but it's hard because I'm a girl." Her voice changed in midspeech, back to the little-girl inflections and strangely voiced question marks.

She did not, in truth, appear girlish but we didn't argue.

"My work was unrecognized at first, you see? No one seemed to understand what I was doing and there were those who criticized me at first. Then I came here. They wouldn't publish my papers and they said the most awful things about me. As if the sexuality exercises . . . but that's a different story. And now everything is going so *well*, you see. Dr. Natelson understood but it's unfortunate. And it is quite a lot of money. So we can't have it, we just can't have it, it seems very clear to me."

"She's crazy as a loon," Kandy whispered.

"I'll be the judge of that!" Melissa said sharply.

"The simplest and best solution is to call the authorities and explain about the accident and let you get back to work," I said. "Don't you agree?"

"But that would ignore the punishment!" she said. "Quick and effective punishment purges guilt and lets the recipient get about the business of living. It is a concept too frequently ignored or ridiculed. They laughed at some of my ideas for papers, you know. Punishment."

"And what punishment do you have in mind?" I asked. "Staying after school and doing the blackboards?"

"Oh, no," she said brightly. "I think, yes, drowning would be appropriate in this case."

She waved the gun at me roguishly.

What about six Hail Marys and six Our Fathers?

33

ONE MIGHT ARGUE THAT death by drowning was not a punishment that allows the punished person to "get about the business of living," but the contradiction did not seem to bother Melissa in the slightest.

As one who devoured Saturday morning Fun Club movies at a great rate when a teenager, I remember somebody, Randolph Scott maybe, patting his holstered .45 and calling it "the equalizer." Melissa's gun, although hardly as potent as the Old West hawgleg, had that effect here. I would not have considered Melissa a serious physical threat in other circumstances, even though she was a big woman. Male muscle versus female, a lifetime of physical competition, macho ego-matching, all that. But thirty ounces of blued metal made all the difference.

If the radical fems really wanted equality, or a touch

more, maybe they should all start packing iron. Maybe they do.

Perhaps somewhere, deep in our rooted psyches, the physical difference *was* the difference, buried and unnoticed, but real. I certainly could empathize with a 110-pound female person in the company of a large male, always, subliminally, aware that she was physically at a disadvantage. God, how I could empathize.

"Oh, shit, you don't want to do that," I said bravely.

"No," Kandy said soothingly, "you really don't want to drown Beaumont. He's too . . ." Her voice trailed off. Come on, Kandy, I'm too what? Think of something! Cute, stimulating, handy for changing light bulbs. Cuddly.

"It's a *perfect* solution. You too, of course," Melissa replied. She was shifting into a new gear, her eyes sparkled and she achieved the semipatronizing style of the babysitter. She also had a .32 automatic and I had become a strong advocate of gun control. Kandy looked shocked and speechless.

"Where we caught those tarpon, remember?" Melissa was being patient and reasonable and I caught a measuring look from Kandy. I believe I had glossed over my personal experiences with Melissa and felt guilty for it, although sexual encounters in the past seemed pointless now.

"Now, I don't want to hear any argument," Melissa said decisively. "Your boat is in the water?"

I nodded and she suggested we get going immediately.

"Hell, you don't want to do that, not if you want to go to Pass Cavallo," I told her. "We'll run over something in the dark or get lost or whatever."

"But I can't take you out there when people can see my gun, in the daylight. Besides I need to get back to work." Take out the garbage, straighten up the house, unplug the coffeepot, kill Beaumont, and go to work, right?

"Me too? Why?" Kandy asked finally and logically.

"I need sweet little Tammy here because I feel she is

really responsible for Dr. Natelson meeting his accident," Melissa told her. "And I certainly don't want all the fuss and bother you could cause."

"Oh, I won't." We were all humoring the lady with the gun and not making a good job of it. Melissa was still as attuned to nuance and posture and inflection as a lifetime of listening and analyzing data can make a person. Maybe she had flipped, but we weren't going to fool her, not about anything important like who gets drowned this morning. Melissa favored Kandy with a "sure" look and smiled. We were going to do it her way.

"Look," I said. "Uh, you can take me out there, but I believe it would be better, for the accident, if you left both girls here. They could . . . explain the accident better."

"Please remember, Beaumont, that I am a doctor. I can explain the accident perfectly well. Now I want you to take Tammy and secure her."

"Secure her how?"

"Tie her with your boat-person knots, of course. To the stove would be adequate."

Tammy, who had been mostly silent, started screeching. No way would we tie her, no sir. She had no intention of staying here with the body. Melissa was fuckin' crazy, it wasn't her fault, she had nothing to do with any of this and she was leaving. We were all crazy.

I wished she'd quit throwing that word around, remembering from someplace that the one thing you didn't want to tell a crazy person is that she was crazy. My hushing got us nowhere and Tammy was working herself up to a middlin' size fit and it was getting near to three o'clock in the morning and I was bone-tired. Probably I'd feel more sympathetic if I was slated for a two-way boat trip.

Melissa, perhaps seasoned by a lifetime of dealing with fits, let Tammy's words wash over her. She walked close and put a hand on Tammy's shoulder and did something and the screeching stopped in midsentence and Tammy slumped to the ground.

"Carotid artery," Melissa said. "Tie her up please."

Bondage games in the early A.M. I found some nylon cord and did some loose hitches around Tammy's wrists. Then I redid them because Melissa inspected my work and found it wanting. Finally, we agreed that it would be best to put her in the bedroom and Kandy and I picked her up, under the gun, and carried her in there. Poor kid. I suspect she'd be anorexic *and* bulemic if we ever got out of this mess.

Melissa also found a vial in her purse and gave her some sort of pill, assuring us that it was merely a mild sedative. I wished for one myself.

There are too many TV shows with guns and gangsters and bad guys holding people against their will. Adult education. Each step of the way, Melissa considered where we were and how to immobilize us, or at least make it difficult for us to attack, while she made her Tammy-arrangements. Hands on the wall, weight on the wall, spread the legs. Lie facedown. Sit in the corner with Kandy on my lap, an arrangement I normally would welcome.

I saw no chance to bop her and get out of this.

And we knew she'd use the gun.

I was glad Kandy was wearing jeans instead of shorts.

When my son was very young, he evolved a remarkably efficient method of dealing with crisis, in his case the pediatrician and shots. Upon entering the doctor's office, he would immediately fall asleep, knowing that a booster shot was forthcoming. The needle would come out and the shot be administered and he'd wake up in the car on the way home, none the worse for wear.

Something like this was happening to me now, waiting for the sky to gray up in the east, rocking at anchor just off the mouth of the bay. Melissa had been adamant and we three had ambled down to the boat, cast off, and burbled slowly out of the slip, the only witness a scrawny cat that survived on scraps and bait shrimp flung to her by people loading and unloading their boats. I wanted the smart-ass teenager desperately but he was a no-show at 4 A.M.

I had managed to persuade her that it was foolish to try to run the big bay and do the twelve miles to Pass Cavallo in the darkness. Other than that, I was batting zilch. She sat facing the stern on the forward casting deck. No way to toss her overboard with some bad throttle work or running aground. She made Kandy free the lines back at the slip and then come back to sit in the passenger chair beside me. The bay was calm in the predawn stillness and the pole lights on shore made glowing reflections in the sheeted water.

Kandy anchored us to wait for dawn, and it seemed to take forever for the anchor rode to slip off the bow deck and finally snub us up against the twelve-pound Danforth. Then we rocked peacefully in six-inch seas.

And I kept falling asleep. Hardly a heroic posture.

I think Melissa was doing a doctor version of speed because she showed no inclination to relax. She kept a Winston glowing and discouraged conversation, just sat there with the gun on her knee and watched and waited. At least fifty-three great plans went through my head, ranging from shorting out our riding lights to tossing a wrench. I couldn't see what I'd gain by shorting out the dim bow light and the only wrench handy was a little six-inch crescent I kept on the console to tighten down the damn bolt on the chart recorder that kept coming loose. I had a radio but I doubted she'd let me call a Mayday to the Coast Guard.

About six, it had lightened up enough to see the larger obstructions, and Melissa had me start up and run slowly ahead as Kandy pulled the anchor. She kept the gun at Kandy's back throughout this operation. Back in place, I wheeled the boat around, pointed toward the opening where the little bay enters Matagorda Bay, and slapped the throttles wide open.

My boat is powered by twin counter-rotating Yamaha 230 Specials, which means it's a fishing hotrod. It leaped up on plane with a roar and Melissa momentarily lost her balance and fell sideways. I yanked the wheel hard left, hardly the way to treat a passenger, to accentuate the G-forces, and slapped the steering wheel to indicate to Kandy she should take it. Then I lunged around the console to beat the shit out of our crazy doctor. Not easy work since I had to pull myself forward and Kandy misunderstood and straightened out the boat, which allowed Melissa to catch her balance. She promptly whacked me across the temple with the side of the gun with all the force her nearly six-foot body could muster.

Black noise and shrieks. Engines screaming, tachs must be pegged. Hard chrome grab rail against my face. Somebody shouting something. Wrong side of my face hurting. I was semi-wedged between the side of the console and the forward edge of the front platform in a kneeling position, sticky on the other side of my face. Melissa, when my vision had cleared, was all the way to the bow shouting something and Kandy wasn't watching where we were going. I estimated our speed at close to forty-five knots, too fast. I made patting motions down with my hands and Kandy finally pulled back the throttles too far and we came off plane and started mushing along bow high.

Melissa was still hollering and I made out something about "stupid and clumsy" and I felt both. I hauled my weary old clumsy body upright, nausea flooding in, and went meekly back to the wheel. In about half a minute we were going to smack the big oyster reef outside the mouth of the bay and I didn't want to do that to my hull so I straightened the boat out and edged the throttles forward, ignoring Ms. Tough Guy in the bow.

Hell, I already felt shot and she had told us she wanted

no bullet holes in our corpses. Kandy was crying, looking miserably guilty, and I gave her a pat and said, "Well, it seemed like a good idea." All the gauges and instruments read fine and the engines hummed along sweetly at about four thousand. I synched everything up and saluted the bow.

I figured we'd be at the Pass in about twenty minutes, still not full daylight, and I wanted to get there as quickly as possible. Once clear of the spoil dumps around the Alcoa Channel I edged up to forty-five hundred on the tachs and headed toward the Pass, no happy fishing anticipation this time. Despite the cold hours in the dark, I felt very alive and awake, steady drip of adrenaline in my blood, eyes keen, hands steady, not at all like a person with a future measured in hours. I felt good, sharp with a background of terror. The sky in the east was full of puffy clouds on the horizon, beginning to rim with a reddish glow from the rising sun.

"We're late, we're late, for a very important date," I sang, and Kandy looked at me like *I* was crazy. Melissa had accepted the current status quo and was back in her perch on the bow. With gun, what the *au courant* murderer needs.

34

THE TEXAS COAST CURVES down in a giant arc beginning at the Louisiana border and ending at the Mexican. The land orientation goes from almost due east and west to almost due north and south. The lower coast is roughly the same latitude as Miami without the highly publicized drug wars. Our drug wars are at the moment undiscovered by the major national media.

Port O'Connor sits roughly in the middle of this curve and is typical of the coast in that it offers a series of thin barrier islands behind which an intricate network of bays and inlets, mostly quite shallow and all blazingly hot in summer, have grown up. It's a disappointing coast in some ways. The outflow from the Mississippi River creates countless tons of silt and sand, which ocean currents send over to Texas and which make most of the Gulf waters easily roiled. Except at the southern tip, the Laguna Madre, the bays are generally not terribly clear and are surrounded by flatlands, brown dirt where mainly mesquite trees and sawgrass grow. Our beaches tend to the brown, rocky cliffs and pounding waves are largely absent. The terrain does have a certain rugged beauty, frequently compared to the surface of the moon.

I love it.

Between the islands and peninsulas that protect the bay systems, there are a number of major passes to the ocean. These allow a periodic tidal flushing of the bays, fresh Gulf water bringing with it renewed life, plankton, small fish to attract the larger predators, the endless complexities of the food chain. San Luis Pass between Galveston and Freeport and Pass Cavallo at Port O'Connor are two of the biggest.

On each tidal change billions of tons of seawater rush through the passes, creating currents and eddies, riptides, sandbars, the "undertow" of folklore, which is nothing more than a strong current running parallel to the beach and, occasionally, a fisherman's paradise. Melissa and I had caught the tarpon of Pass Cavallo on a day like that so many months before. She had obviously remembered my impromptu lecture about the dangers of the Pass, the vicious currents, the ever-changing structure of the bottom, and the friend I had who stepped in a hole wadefishing and they never did find the body.

That's where we were headed and it was getting much too light for my taste. "Shooting light," the duck hunters would say. I edged the throttles up again and we raced past the sleepy little town of Port O'Connor, the rich folks' homes facing the bay and the infrastructure folks' homes blocked out by them. On our left a quarter mile or so was Matagorda peninsula, a half-mile wide would be stretching it, and ahead lay Matagorda Island. Between the two low spits of sand was Pass Cavallo, maybe a mile and a half wide and full of the nastiest sandbars you've ever torn-up a lower unit upon. Also sharks, sting rays, Portuguese men o' war, riptides, huge holes, tricky channels, and deserted beaches.

I avoided out of the habit the big sand flat, which averages about four inches deep and which lies across most of the bay side of the Pass, and skirted the peninsula at about fifty yards, which looks scary the first time you do it but there was a good deep channel parallel to the beach and I had checked every yard of it with my LCD depth finder long ago. We broke out into the Pass and Melissa was waving from the bow, making mouth motions I chose not to hear above the engines, and I was pleased to see the weather guy got it right, the tide was indeed ebbing as advertised. The irresistible force of the outgoing tide battled against the prevailing wind and breakers from the Gulf. I was forced to back down by the swells, a confused sea, a whitecapping mess. Big waves were stacking up on the several bars that the endless currents had formed and the wind had come up with the light and was blowing spray off the top of the breakers. Green Gulf water fought a losing battle against the outgoing tide and milky bay water mingled and mixed with it in streaks. There wasn't another boat in sight and Melissa was getting serious with the gun.

I was standing at the wheel and after we hit the first couple of good waves, much splashing, sheets of water thrown from the bow, Kandy stood up too, holding onto the grab rail I had installed for the passenger. Melissa was having a tougher time of it, her position in the bow accentuating the pitching of the boat. I backed down another notch automatically as we began to clear the Pass and edge toward the Gulf. Melissa scrambled back, waving the gun, and I wondered if she had reconsidered her position vis-à-vis bullet holes. Naturally there wasn't another boat, not a camper, Park Patrol, or even an offshore helicopter in sight. I could see a white line of breakers on both sides and a confused sea. I pointed the bow toward the big sand bar which parallels the beach.

It felt like the desert, lonely and primeval, and I nodded, grabbed Kandy's arm, and dove over the side, after making one final adjustment with the wheel that should have Melissa firmly aground in about thirty seconds. I also slapped both throttles wide open and the boat jumped forward as I was jumping sideways.

I took most of the impact on my butt and back.

Water does not compress and I suspect we were doing something over twenty miles an hour when we exited, so the overall effect was similar to jumping out of a moving car onto hard clay. It hurt. I had wrapped arms and legs around a startled and struggling Kandy and was able to shield her somewhat, but she had no time to fill her lungs and she was choking and gasping and sputtering when I finally got us straightened out, treading water, maybe three hundred yards from the beach, as unreachable as the moon.

We were being bounced around by the waves a good bit. I would have thought it calm, except in the water even a little chop seems monumental. Salt water though, good flotation. It stung my eyes and I kept getting mouthfuls when I talked. The outgoing tides had created currents that I estimated were over three knots and you can't swim across that, not in street clothes and ordinary condition, not with a 110-pound girl to help.

Said girl seemed somewhat upset with me. "You didn't even ask if I could swim!"

"Can you?"

"Yes, you fucker, why'd you do that!"

"You prefer what she had in mind, maybe?" I gasped. Talking was a chore. I watched the shoreline slide past and knew there was no way we'd reach it. I knew Melissa had fired once and checked to see if I had more than the normal amount of holes in my lanky old carcass. I was okay and I had heard the unmistakable roar of outboard engines tilting up and roaring as she hit the bar out in the middle of the Pass. Jesus, I hoped she hadn't broken anything serious.

"What a guy!" I said to a still-sputtering Kandy.

"Who?"

"Me!"

"Why?"

"Because I just saved your delectable ass and I claim it as my own for the Queen of Spain, her royal majesty. Take off your pants."

"Jesus, Beaumont, you are totally weird." She sputtered and took in some seawater, which meant I had to pound her back, grinning like an idiot.

"This is not due to your considerable sexual charm," I yelled. "We're gonna use them as water wings." Then I struggled out of my old jeans to demonstrate, tying the legs at the feet and whipping them over my head to trap air and using the resulting buoyancy to keep me floating. The open, waist end of the jeans in the water pushed the air up the legs and the fibers held enough to keep you afloat for several minutes before you had to repeat the process. Old Boy Scout trick. And it worked. Which was good since I was tired of treading water and we were getting farther away from land every minute, carried by the relentless tide. Kandy watched this operation, which required submerging several times and the involuntary ingestion of several mouthfuls of seawater, with skepticism but then imitated me.

"We're not going to swim for it?"

"Too much current," I hollered. "Better to let it take us down the beach a ways and then we can sorta body-surf into the beach." I wondered if Melissa could get the boat unstuck and locate us. We were maybe three, four hundred yards away from where we jumped and the boat had gone on a ways before she hit. Probably okay. I felt good.

Even the water felt good, warm and comforting. I tried

to see the boat but couldn't and if I couldn't see her she didn't have a prayer of seeing me, even from a higher elevation. "Hell of a morning for a swim," I yelled to Kandy.

"What about the sharks?" she yelled back. "Won't they eat me?"

"If they won't, I will," I promised.

35

ASIDE FROM THE FACT that my boat
was missing and Sheriff Orton thought I was a deviated
pervert although not pronouncing it quite like that, I was in
fine shape. I didn't even have to go to the Port Lavaca jail
to make a statement, thanks to Evans, who reminded the
sheriff that I had handled his election ad campaign for free.
The entire scene at my bay house had a very urban look to
it, except the people. Lots of cop cars, revolving lights, body
bag, squawk of two-way radios, the whole bit.

Many people in uniforms looking official. Onlookers,
mostly with gimme caps and beer cans. Fat ladies in polyester. You could almost see the story making the rounds,
embellishments added by every person, like a gust of wind
in a cornfield.

Kandy and I were a touch bedraggled, you can't really

blame the sheriff. We had made it to the beach and walked across the half mile of sand to the bay side and waved until a passing boat decided to swing into the shore and pick us up. The guy couldn't understand why I didn't want to go looking for the Grady-White and kept talking about "salvage." I told him I thought that was pertinent to the high seas only and would he mind dropping us off at Port O'Connor? As he reversed away from the dock, you could see the wheels turning, and I'll bet he was heading for Pass Cavallo and my "abandoned" forty-thousand-dollar rig the minute he cleared the little jetties.

Do mind the crazy lady with the gun, now.

For forty bucks, one of the hangers-on drove us over to Point Lookout and Sheriff Orton. Tammy had managed to get free of my purposely clumsy knots and gone to Evans lickety split. He called in the law, Mrs. Evans clucking at about forty CPM, and from then on officialdom took over. They did get rid of the body, that was a break, and the three of us told essentially the same story, so the sheriff had nobody to "a-rest." I gave him a detailed description of the boat, last seen heading toward the big sandbar across the middle of the Pass, lady aboard and her description, wanted for suspicion of homicide.

What the sheriff couldn't understand is why I had *two* ladies down here, and his eyebrows collided with his rather low hairline when Kandy described herself as a "dancer" and Tammy told him she was unemployed. He didn't say the word, not with Mrs. Evans glaring protectively, but it was obvious I was up to no good. *Two* much, thought Sheriff Orton.

I called Vince at the club early on and he agreed he didn't want to miss all the fun, so he loomed up in the doorway at about dinnertime, solidifying all of Sheriff Orton's doubts.

It was dark by the time the last official car left. How do they get batteries that will run those light bars for hours and still start the engine? The police took Natelson's Mercedes. The Evanses took Tammy with them. The Evanses made it very clear that she was under their protection and I think she was grateful for it. She kept telling everybody too much about the late Dr. Natelson, who was rapidly assuming heroic proportions in the telling. In my younger days, I'd have offered a few crude reminders of Dr. Natelson's all-too-humanness, but the urge to correct the world is dying slowly within me. "Beaumont," said Vince, eyeing me over a very light scotch, "you have an absolutely positive genius for fucking up."

"I thought I was rather heroic."

"He saved my life," said Kandy.

"He should have," observed Vince.

"There was no way I could have known she would flip. She's a shrink, for god's sake."

"Adler had a theory of compensation, overcoming problems to excel, the guy with a limp running the mile. Somebody once asked him if that meant that crazy people became shrinks," said Vince. I hate it when he did that. Been at the library again, compensation no doubt for his misspent college years.

"Events got out of control."

"Do we have to stay here?" Kandy's opinion of this was obvious. I wasn't just exactly charmed with the idea of staying at the lonely bay house myself.

"I wonder where she is?" Vince said.

For answer, I went over to the corner and flipped on the highly illegal VHF I kept in the house. Illegal because these radios are for maritime use only. Nowadays, the price of VHF transceivers had got down so low that the world was flooded with them and the owners paid very little attention to FCC rules, which meant that the FCC threw up its governmental hands and ignored the problem mostly. I dialed in the weather band and listened to as nice a forecast as one could ask for: "seas one to three feet, winds southeast at ten knots."

"She could be anywhere. I don't think she's a boat pro but she's obviously very competent and she could have gone out in the Gulf and fumbled her way down the coast or she could be in any of about three thousand square miles of bay. Anywhere."

"The one place she has to come is here," Vince said.

"Why here, she wouldn't want to come back here, for Christ's sake. That'd be dumb."

Kandy's eyes were too wide.

"She has to come here," Vince repeated.

"Why?"

"To kill you, of course. It's her best shot."

I stared at him.

"Pardon the pun," he said calmly.

36

As Vince saw it, it was quite simple.

"Start with the premise that the broad is crazy because of wrong assumptions. If you give her her assumption, everything she does makes sense. Once I got her straightened out, we got along fine." He seemed a touch smug to me, for a guy whose best friend was about to be shot.

"Premise," I said, to retaliate for the business about Adler.

"Premise, assumption, same difference. Her premise is that she has been wronged by you and that you're the guy who can fuck up a very nearly perfect life. Have been doin' it. Kill you . . . solve the problem. Killing's no chore for her, you saw that."

"But Kandy and Tammy saw her shoot Natelson. The magnificent Dr. Natelson you heard about. Jerk."

"Tammy's a patient, patients can be controlled. 'Obviously, suffering from a delusional distortion that alters the reality base.' Kandy's just a broad, a topless dancer. She shows her tits. Whose word would you take?"

"Thanks a lot," said Kandy. He raised his hands in a "not-me" gesture. There was a certain rough logic in what he said. But she would have to arrange it nicely, no chance of the obvious suspicion being confirmed, something like an accidental drowning would work fine. I shivered.

"I would like my boat back."

"Maybe if you ask her nicely," he snorted.

"Maybe *she* drowned," Kandy said.

"Shit, she'd have to work at it," I said. "That boat is damn near idiot-proof. And the weather is calm, she's probably lost somewhere. Tanks were nearly full, she's got a hundred-, hundred-fifty-mile range. With safety margin." Damn, I sounded like a boating safety brochure, not a hero.

"Galveston, Freeport, Port Aransas, she's got a lot of coast to work," Vince said. "Or maybe right outside."

Kandy gave a little shriek and announced she was going to a motel. She disappeared into the bedroom to pack, presumably. Vince smiled a sleepy smile at me. "Why don't we just kinda wait around and see what happens?"

"Jesus, Vince, I don't want to do that. This isn't a deer blind and I have no desire to be a hunter."

"You," he said, "are the bait."

We talked Kandy out of the motel idea and buttoned her up in the bedroom. We then got out the Off and took a bath in it. Then we went out to the deck, after Vince made a trip to the Lincoln and came back with a massive-looking automatic.

"You just slapped her around before," I whispered.

"That was before she started shooting people."

I thought this was a job for Sheriff Orton and told him so. The mosquitoes would whine in for the kill and then catch a whiff of Off and buzz away. I swear their doppler-buzz sounded disappointed. I kept falling asleep, not good technique for bait.

And, of course, the night was as peaceful and quiet as you could ask. A blazing canopy of stars blinked at us and I would have been inspired to compose some poetry if that didn't seem inappropriate. I don't think Vince was similarly moved. He sat in the corner, chair tilted back, as silent and menacing as a Gila monster. With blond hair, of course. Probably reviewing the psychoanalytic theories of Adler and Jung.

I snuck over and asked how he could stay awake.

"Learned it when I was on the cops," he whispered back. "Just let yourself think."

I tried that but my tired brain just flopped around. I didn't know he'd been a cop. There were a number of gaps between the time we ran around in high school until the day I walked into his club and accidentally stopped a drunk patron and robber from cold-cocking him from behind.

I wondered if Melissa had any Off. Probably back in Houston calling lawyers. Probably stuck out in the marsh, in which case I hoped she found the bug repellant in the console. Some things are too horrible even for murderers.

I was sound asleep when Vince got up, yawned and stretched and announced that his baby-sitting fee was four eggs scrambled and lots of bacon and sausage and what did I plan to do about it? I managed to handle that, waking up a tired Kandy in the process, and we had breakfast about eight feet from where Natelson's body had been last night.

That's a commentary on something. Probably scrambled eggs.

After we finished, I stacked the dishes and Vince ran a big hand over his stubble and announced he was going to hit the road. "Maybe I guessed wrong," he said.

"Maybe she saw you-all," Kandy said nervously.

"Why don't you go back with him? Just move into my place over on Richmond back in Houston. 'Executive Housing.' It's not too bad. I think my American Express still works."

"What are you gonna do?"

"I'm back to business as usual. Got clients to take care of. Ads to write. Campaigns to sell. Got to get some business, the checkbook's getting thin."

"I suspect you'll have some depositions to make," Vince said, finishing his fourth cup of coffee.

"That too."

Kandy agreed to catch a ride with Vince, rather too readily for my taste, and he napped while she packed. In thirty minutes I waved good-bye. I really didn't feel like being there by myself and I was ashamed of the feeling. Six-two of macho male worried about a girl! "But it's one hell of a girl," I said aloud. Last seen mad and homicidal in Pass Cavallo. Aground in Pass Cavallo. I took my nap in the spare bedroom with the curtains drawn and a chair propped under the doorknob.

Long about lunchtime, Evans came to wake me up. Actually he came by to do me another favor, adding to a total I'd never balance out.

"Let's go looking for the boat," he said. "Mamma and Tammy are going to town."

"How's she doing?"

"Mamma's fine," he said shortly. And Tammy's better away from you, I added for him.

"I don't ask for this sort of shit," I explained. "And I certainly didn't mean to . . . I'm not responsible for . . ."
He waved me to silence.

He did let me make some coffee and pour the scalding brew down my gullet and we were out in his bay shrimper in a half hour. He used an oversize version of a jonboat, eighteen by eight feet, seventy horsepower, adorned with shrimp net, plywood culling box, and a rusty hatchet for debating with stingrays and alligator gars. It was a noisy and rough-riding rig and I was glad the weather was holding and the bay had barely a ripple. We streaked across the empty expanse of Matagorda Bay in fine style. With the breeze whipping at my face I felt inordinately fine and rummaged in the ice chest to find a cold pop top, which tasted like heaven right here on earth. Even with the fishy smell.

I liked this trip a lot more than the previous and vowed silently that there would be no impromptu swimming this time. The boat was not on the sandbar in the middle, where I had last seen it, and I hollered that she had obviously got it off.

"What would she do?" Evans asked.

He was asking me to get into the mind of a female. A female doctor, a shrink and a killer, driven by god knows what, a woman I had been intimate with but didn't know.

"Inside," I shouted. "She'd stay inside." How much my reasoning was influenced by not wishing to go out in the Gulf in a jonboat, I cannot say. But it seemed reasonable, the Gulf is a scary place indeed for the nonboatperson. Or a boatperson, given a touch of bad weather.

He nodded and swung the boat around and we headed toward Espiritu Santo Bay, Dewberry Island, and the innumerable grassy sloughs and cuts and bayous that formed the interlocking bay systems on the inside of Pass Cavallo. We poked our nose into each little inlet and bay and cove, Evans silent and poker faced at the wheel, me up in the bow with his rusty 7×35 binoculars.

Forty-eleven things could have happened to the boat. One of the hard-faced illegal netters could have come upon it in the middle of the night and it would then see nocturnal service, scarred and smashed, burdened with monofilament nets and always an eye for the wardens. Or a fisherman could have made a forty-thousand-dollar catch, twenty-five feet of trophy to be towed in and perhaps reported, perhaps not. Or it could be out in the Gulf, drifting along at the mercy of the wind and the waves, waiting to be shoved by ocean currents down to Mexico or washed up on a deserted beach and pounded to pieces in the next squall.

"We need a chopper," I hollered after forty-five minutes of nothing.

He motioned me to keep looking and we rounded a point, the outboard skeg dragging a trail behind us, just barely planing so as to soften the impact if we ran aground. The sun was at the blister stage in the midafternoon and the calm waters threw off a thousand glints and glares, blinding me in the binoculars.

He ran us up on a sandbar once and we had to get out and shove, shuffling our feet automatically to kick up any sleeping stingrays. Mullet swirled out ahead of us and occasionally we'd see a bigger fish blasting something along the grassy shorelines and we hadn't seen another boat in an hour. Grimly Evans continued to check out each pocket of water.

And we found the thing, canted over to the side, one engine tilted up, looking empty on an oyster reef hard aground in the middle of a nameless cove about two miles from the middle of Pass Cavallo. I hadn't even looked for the silver swirl of tarpon, I remembered.

"Be careful," I yelled over the motor. "She was fairly hostile last time I saw her and I'm sure a night on the bay didn't improve her temper."

He nodded and slid out a rusty shotgun from the console, jacked a shell into the chamber, and laid it on the seat. Evans had flown and fought in several wars and had no intention of turning the other cheek.

We circled the Grady-White at dead slow, checking it out, and she wasn't aboard. Unless she was hiding in the fishbox. But no dramatics were necessary, just boat maintenance. The oyster reef had gouged several new scrapes in the hull and the primary battery was dead. I figured she had got stuck, tried to pull off with the engines, which would stall when the props encountered unyielding shell. Starting and restarting is the quickest way to drain a battery, and she wouldn't have known about the twin battery setup and the switch that let her draw on both. Perhaps my lectures about sharks and stingrays had taken hold and kept her from getting into the water to free the boat. She could have walked to the shore along the reef, I was surprised she hadn't seen it sticking out into the bay. Bad boatmanship, Dr. Stone.

Evans held the nose of his boat against the reef and I jumped out and waded over to mine, anxious and worried about the damage. It was the only worry I could do something about, so I focused on it. I flipped the battery switch to "Both" and had power, raised the other motor and tried to shove the thing backward off the shell. No go. Evans was untying his anchor line to use as a tow rope and I cleated it off on the stern of my boat. He tied off on his stern, idled over until he had a straight pull, and mashed the throttle. The line whipped taut through the water, throwing spray, and I pushed from the bow and we slid off with much scraping, grinding, and rasping, me clinging to the bow until I could scramble aboard.

I pulled the hatches and checked the bilge to see that everything was okay, and it was dry as a bone. The bottom of the Grady-White resembles a battleship's plating. I had one badly nicked prop and assorted scratches, lots of mud on the decks from people getting in and out, but both engines started. I ran a check on all the systems aboard, Evans circling patiently in his boat, and finally put the things into gear and eased out in the deeper waters, feeling myself again. I motioned for him to lead the way and we headed home.

The boat had a bad vibration on the starboard engine over 4000 RPM and I figured I was in the market for a new four-hundred-dollar stainless prop. Other than that, it was fine, and I dipped a bucket over the side and washed some of the mud out the scuppers in the transom.

"Damn, I'm glad to see you," I told the boat. We negotiated the passes and the shallows carefully and broke out into the deep water of Matagorda in half an hour. Evans led the way and I planed along beside him, our wakes curling out back straight as a ruler, mingling on the placid surface of the big bay.

The ammeter on the dash said the primary battery was taking a lot of charge and momentarily I thought about wiring my brain into the circuit.

Where in the hell was she?

37

Evans waved and went on down to his pier and I motored cautiously up into the slip and tied off to the rotten pier. The lady who owned the slip kept promising to rebuild the piers, one of which was sagging into the water, but she hadn't and you had to pick your way cautiously, avoiding loose boards and outright holes. The locals made book on how many tipsy fishermen would slip and take a header on a given weekend. I had provided many chuckles by trying to help an unfortunate whose bow was stuck in the mud on an exceptionally low tide by bracing my feet against one of the uprights and falling face first into the mud when it gave way.

A thousand laughs, that's Beaumont.

Evans drove up by the time I had backed the trailer

down the ramp preparing to load the boat out and was winching that heavy bastard up on it.

"Hey. You're just in time. Come turn this thing a minute," I panted over the winch handle.

He came over, stood too close to me, said quietly, "Mamma's asleep. But Tammy's gone."

"Where?"

"I don't know. Her purse is on my dining-room table."

"She out walkin'?"

"She'd walk down here, wouldn't she? I drove over the rest of the places she'd go. She's not there. And Sarah never takes a nap in the afternoon. Never. She's not up to your place, is she?"

"No. What are you telling me?"

"Come on back and let's wake up the wife and find out."

I reversed the ratchet and let the Grady-White slide back down the trailer, avoiding the spinning winch handle. When she was afloat again, I quickly tied off bow and stern on a pier out of the way. Then I jumped into the Blazer and hauled the trailer back to my place, left truck and trailer there, and hopped in Evans's pickup. We drove to his house in silence.

Inside, he went back into the bedroom and emerged with a very groggy Mrs. Evans. She acted drunk and the lady rarely took a drink. Last thing she remembered is that she and Tammy had come back from their shopping and were having a glass of ice tea from the pitcher in the fridge. Then she got so sleepy she just had to lie down for a minute. That was an hour and a half ago, as best she could remember. Tammy was napping on the couch.

In Point Lookout, one rarely locks anything. Homes were left open as a matter of course, parked cars had ignition keys in them, and people watched over each other's stuff. My boat once was being hauled to Port Lavaca for service and the boat guy used a new pickup and was stopped twice before he got a mile from my place by residents who recognized my boat but not the pickup hauling it. It was no big deal to walk into somebody's house. Or open the fridge and take your chances with the ice tea pitcher.

"Are you thinking what I'm thinking?" Evans asked.

I nodded. Asked Mrs. Evans if she felt normal, or was she—

"I feel like I have a hangover. I remember having a hangover, in Galveston, when we—you remember, Burt." He nodded and blushed, so help me. Mrs. Evans smiled at him.

"How 'bout some coffee," I suggested, and she agreed and bustled off to make it. I would have done it but she would not tolerate strangers in the kitchen, a rule I learned early on when I attempted to wash dishes after having dinner with them. Mrs. Evans was a feminist, in a way, very sure of her own worth and independent where it counted. She was also a homemaker, melding both roles in a strange Point Lookout way, and you didn't mess in her kitchen.

"I think she's gone," Evans said bluntly.

"I think you're right."

"This has gone beyond anything we can handle, boy," he said. "I'm going to call Orton again. There's been one murder here, the first ever, and Tammy's a witness." He walked over to the phone and paused, looking at me. "Damn it, Beaumont, why you get in all these messes . . . just messes."

"I didn't try to, didn't plan it, you know."

"I know. But we both love that girl so much and I'm worried about her. Her and you are over, right?"

"Yes."

He made a sour-mouth and called. I picked up on his introductory lines and then Mrs. Evans came in with three coffees and I took the tray from her and made her sit down. Evans wasn't talking much, doing a lot of listening. I heard him say "no" a couple of times, one "that's stupid," and then he hung up.

"Maybe there's more mess here than we thought," he said slowly. Then he sipped his coffee and looked directly at me. "John Orton says he's supposed to pick you up."

"For what, for Christ sakes!" But I knew. I knew exactly what that bitch had done and I was heading for the phone even as Evans was saying "The lady-doctor got some high-priced Houston lawyers leaning on the po-lice up there and they want to talk to you about the murder of Dr. Henry Natelson."

"Vince," I said into the phone. "Is Kandy still with you?"

38

VINCE AND I SNARLED at each other on the phone, underlying fear putting an edge on words spoken too hastily. I thought you called her, that's what she said and she's heading your direction, should be there by now, he said. God almighty, why'd you let her go? Because you called, stupid. I didn't call, don't you know that crazy lady's out there somewhere scheming? If you had. I didn't start. You were responsible. You took her back to Houston. But you.

None of this was gaining us anything and I outlined the situation here, reported again that I had not seen any sign of Kandy and I had recovered the boat but no Dr. Stone.

And that the Houston cops wanted me, oh boy! It was my first time as a suspect, a perp, and I didn't like it, nameless fears boiling underneath an all-too-sharp memory of my drug dream when Dr. Stone was jerking my head around.

"I'll come down," Vince said.

"No, hell, I think we'd be better off with you there. I'll poke around here and see if I can dodge the sheriff long enough to find out what that crazy bitch is after. Hell, they might throw *you* in jail."

"Beaumont," he said. "If she gets you now . . . she's got *all* the cards."

"Well, we'll just have to protect my delicate little hide, now won't we?"

"Just remember. You're the last witness and the only person who can ruin what she's built up over the past ten-fifteen years. The lady is highly motivated."

"And very ingenious and quick with a hypo, I know."

"She ain't doing too bad, thus far," he pointed out as he hung up. Evans had out the house shotgun, as opposed to the boat shotgun, and was checking its chamber.

"What's your plan?" he asked as he jacked a shell into the chamber. Evans was a direct man.

"Simple. I'm going to go be bait," I told them.

"Want me to . . ." And I waved him off. Lord knows he'd done enough, and the idea of some harm coming to Mrs. Evans was enough to chill anybody's soul. No way.

"You guys stick tight. I'm sure Tammy's okay, she's of no use to the doctor lady dead. If she still wants to negotiate." I didn't believe myself, why should they?

And we had another argument, wasting time again! until I got them to agree the best thing to do was to stall the sheriff and that could be accomplished if the two of them got in the pickup and went to town to see him. Out of the line of fire, admittedly, but Mrs. Evans was definitely a civilian. "You owe it to her," I said. "And to me. Scoot!"

Then I went back to my cabin and fixed myself a truly staggering bourbon. Strong medicine for strong disease. The dark seemed a long time coming although I wasn't through with the drink when the giant red ball of the sun touched the horizon and started to sink. I pulled back curtains and blinds and turned on every light in the place and sat down to wait. I had trouble concentrating on the book I was reading, tensing up at every noise outside and reminding myself that I wanted to be seen and wanted her here. I put Mr. Coffee on and alternated between the brew and the bourbon. Might as well be a wide-awake drunk.

I had lost every round even when I thought I was winning. The Evanses had promised to stay the night in town and it was a weekday so we probably wouldn't have any flounderers rattling down the road to the slip with their flat-bottomed rigs and Coleman lanterns, some converted aircraft lights, gigs, and lots of bug repellant and high hopes.

No matter. I was going to put a stop to this shit.

I was alone and felt it. Probably too quick to turn down Vince. Could have borrowed Evans's shotgun but this was not the OK Corral. It was like being in an aquarium, all lights and no curtains. Why did I have to fight with such a respectable killer? Better a no-name thug, beetle browed and thirty-seven previous arrests, not a nationally respected headshrinker. What set her off? Was it sex that got me into trouble? An inability to relate well? A nosy nose?

"Did I hurt your boat, darling?"

That I didn't jump more than a yard or so I attribute to the fact that I was three-quarters expecting her given the basic validity of Vince's scenario. She looked good, rested and relaxed and no weapons in sight. Simple tailored Guess jeans and a magenta man-tailored shirt and—wonder of wonders—ladylike undergarments that mounded her chest. I regretted that. I motioned her inside, wondering where the car was. Could the unfamiliar bra be a concession to the situation, new image?

"Busted prop, a little vibration, nothing major."

"I'm glad, I suppose, knowing the almost anthropomorphic love you have for the boat. You were quite clever, I thought."

"Necessity is . . . I suppose this is the denouement?"

"This is get-back-to-business. The accident must be accounted for and the authorities must fill out their forms and go through their formalities and we must devise a plan to make this as painless as possible."

"Melissa. It was no accident," I said as she lighted a cigarette.

"But it *was*. He was my partner, after all, a part of the work I must do."

"I think you call that 'denial.' You pointed your gun at him and pulled the trigger *bang!* He was dead. Then you forced me and Kandy out to the boat and you planned to drown us."

"These are typical paranoid suspicions. You need to see a good therapist, darling."

"Where are the girls?"

"None of your concern at the moment. It is you I must deal with? You are the key?"

She seemed so reasonable, controlled and relaxed, and I thought of the gut-grinding anxiety she must be suppressing. Somewhere in her twisted head, the truth was sitting, struggling to emerge, but she showed no sign. And her accomplishments over the last, what? thirty hours? Amazing.

Her hands were behind her back and she leaned against the door frame, letting in bugs. No purse. Hardly anyplace to conceal a gun, although I suppose she could have something tucked into the waistband of the jeans in back.

Her short hair was in place, makeup on, eyes level and unblinking. I had seen eyes like that before, on one of the ramshackle cats that roamed around, as he stalked a bird. I couldn't fly away, more's the pity.

"What is it that you have in mind?" I asked.

"Accidental death. My lawyers say it's an obvious legal possibility. Death by misadventure. We were involved in a dispute, a struggle, Dr. Natelson attempted to reach the weapon and it discharged, unfortunate but unavoidable. I was a psychiatric backup, merely a witness."

"And the real witnesses?"

"Are accounted for. You plead guilty to . . . accidental manslaughter or whatever they call it, the legal terminology irritates me, and get a suspended sentence and we can get about our lives. There will be a consideration for your inconvenience. Perhaps a marketing director's position, six figures, perks, your choice of luxury automobile."

"Whoa. You mean . . ." And I couldn't help laughing. "You mean *I'm* the guy with the gun now? How do you possibly think, what sort of stupid idea is this, *you* had the gun. Luxury automobile? *You* shot Natelson." For a minute I wondered what kind of car you got for perjury in a murder case. A Yugo for DWI, Buick for assault and.

"It was an accident!" she hissed.

"Like hell. You flipped and went bonkers and blasted him right here and I spent an hour scrubbing the bloodstains off the floor and no matter what shit you've cooked up back in Houston you know and I know that you did it. Jesus! I saw you. You're nuts! There are witnesses. You've flipped!" Suddenly I remembered what you're never supposed to tell a crazy person.

"Really, Melissa," I went on in calmer tones, "this is not something you can cover with a fabricated story. But I'm sure something can be worked out." I didn't believe it, I didn't even sound like I believed it. Maybe Famous Liars School. "Let's call Sheriff Orton and your lawyers and arrange a meeting, where we can talk the whole thing out. I'll make it sound as best as I can for you. Temporary insanity or something."

"Laymen! You act like you have some sort of choice," she said harshly. "I offered you an accommodation. You act like you're not responsible."

"I'm *not* responsible. You had the gun and did the shooting. I suppose you washed your hands fifty times but I wonder if a paraffin test wouldn't still show it. You did it, Melissa!"

"Quite a structured delusion," she said in her doctor voice.

"Oh, for god's sake!"

"The patient has constructed a paradigm incorporating a basic reality flaw and is operating under it."

"Knock it off!"

"A continued psychopharmacological therapy program based on lithium derivatives is recommended on an indefinite basis in conjunction with intensive group and individual therapy." Her eyes weren't completely focused and she spoke in a monotone. "Should resistance be encountered it may become necessary to restrain and tranquilize the patient in order to ensure the safety of peers and fellow patients."

"Would you stop this bullshit?"

"The therapist must seek a commonality of agreement in any sphere in order to establish contact and lead the patient back into normalcy."

"You're the one who did the killing!"

"Negative transference is common and is best ignored in favor of seeking such commonalities."

And she began to advance on me, bringing with her a long glistening needle like some absurd horror movie. Dr. Stone was a large person and her body, once so soft and yielding, had grown tense, tendons in the neck standing out, smooth muscles bunched in the forearms under the fine layer of hair. Psychobabble issued from her mouth in a drone. The needle must have been encased somehow at her back. What devil's concoction was in it was anybody's guess.

I didn't bother to reason with her anymore, I think she had gone fugue on me, and I reached out and slapped the shit out of her with one hand while twisting her wrist with my other. I took the expected kick on my thigh, turning into her, trying to hold the hand with the needle clear of my precious, if slightly frayed, body.

She was frighteningly strong. She twisted in my grip, bringing pressure against the thumb, jabbing again and again with her knee. A weird mixture of professional jargon spilled from her lips, along with flecks of foam. If she got one of those knee shots in I'd bend right into her needle. I slapped my other hand on her arm, twisted and got it behind her in a hammerlock.

I was frightened, angry, and still some stupid prohibition kept me from decking her as I should.

"Calm down, goddamn it!" She kicked backward and got me painfully on the shin.

Stubby Horce appeared in the doorway and I said the immortal words first uttered by General Custer, "Oh, shit." Of course she'd have reinforcements, socially destructive impulses channeled into a productive life bashing heads for Dr. Stone, what a deal! He had red polyester shorts and the inevitable running shoes, did not look pleased. He roared when he saw I had the boss at a disadvantage.

I slammed Melissa against the wall hard, the whole cabin shook, and backed away. She slid down the wall to the floor and I figured I could ignore her for a second or two. The stubby bastard was enraged at my treatment of the boss and came lunging across the room, me backing up as fast as I could. Since the room was only twenty feet long, my alternatives were limited.

His pig eyes glowed red as he launched himself at me.

39

I REMEMBER THINKING I should be glad he didn't have a weapon. Then I remembered his painful, playful grip on my shoulder muscles and realized he didn't *need* a weapon. Hurt them fast and first, Vince said.

When my butt hit the kitchen counter I grabbed for the coffee and threw the whole half pot in his ugly face. It was hot enough to make him yell and I smashed the glass pot down on his face and wished for something heavier. Pyrex glass, didn't break. What a testimonial!

Melissa was attempting to get up on the other side of the room, needle still in hand. Why hadn't it smashed? Time had slowed down and I saw things very clearly and in a semi-slo mo. Horce clubbed at me, caught me on the shoulder, which went numb. I could still use the arm, just no feeling, and I smashed my clenched fist at his face, he blocked and I slithered sideways to avoid his terrifying hands. I needed something heavy to hit the sunbitch with. Where was Evans and the trusty shotgun? Melissa had reached a leaning position and was yelling something and again I regretted the solitude and privacy available at Point Lookout. Surely somebody could hear the ruckus.

I shoved my chair in front of his next charge and he got tangled up and fell to his knees and I made a serious attempt to kick him through the wall, unsuccessful since it glanced off his arm, and I swiped backhand at Melissa's stomach and connected. On the short term I was doing fine but the odds were not favorable so I took the time to make sure Melissa was out of it, another whack in the belly, explosion of air from her lungs, there were better things to do with that belly.

Horce was up and roaring and I darted through the door to the porch, stepped sideways, grabbed the cast net that hung by the door on the porch to dry and waited for him to emerge.

A cast net is a universal device, used by virtually all people who feed from the sea. It may be depicted in paintings from the Mayans for all I know. It's a circular net, from two to eight feet in diameter or larger, with lead weights sewn along the perimeter. Strings are connected to the edges and threaded through a hole in the center. In use, you swirl the net out in front of you so it opens up into a circle and lands over the baitfish you're chasing. The lead weights take the edges to the bottom quickly and you draw up the net with the strings. Mine was an eight footer and you grabbed it in the center with the weights at the bottom so I had something heavy, all right, the equivalent of a four-foot lead pipe. Why do we say lead pipe, you hardly ever see pipes made of lead.

When dumbshit came blasting through the door, blindly raging to tear out my lungs, I took a full swing with the net and smashed the weights, forty-eight of them if I remembered correctly, in his ugly face. I might as well have used a lead pipe because he dropped like a shot. My cast net had something like a pound and a half of lead at the bottom, swung with four feet of leverage, plus nice nylon webbing to cut his face. He was twitching and moaning on the floor of the porch.

Then I did something I'm not terribly proud of. I jumped up and landed the full 190 pounds of Beaumont on his right hand, heels first. All sorts of cracking and crunching. Nasty thing to do. Chalk it up to fear.

"Lucky I'm wearing boat shoes," I said defensively. My voice sounded strange and high-pitched. I couldn't get oxygen into my lungs. My face hurt where something had got me. I thought about kicking him in the face a time or two but didn't have the balls. I bent over from the waist, keeping my legs out of his reach—God, I was afraid of him even now—to access the damage.

About that time Melissa came flying through the door, needle first, and got me in the lower back. I slapped back at her hand and the needle came out of my back, drops squirting into the air.

"Shit!" I hollered, facing her. She didn't like what she saw and fled down the stairs, half falling and half running, me in what you call your hot pursuit. I figured I had about three minutes of rationality left, depending on how much of what crap she had stuck me with.

I was too mad to be scared.

As I hit the ground, Melissa with a ten-foot lead, I saw Evans's pickup jolt to a halt in front of my house and he was jumping out, mouth open shouting something I couldn't hear and I set out to catch that bitch and stuff her hypodermic up whatever orifice was handy.

I have long legs but Melissa *was* highly motivated and she maintained her lead, probably trying for the Mercedes, which was parked down by the pier, and I hadn't felt anything from the drugs yet. Maybe adrenaline.

Evans brought up the rear, a poor third. Every yard had a mercury vapor light and we raced through glowing pools of blue and scary shadows. The piers and slip and ramp were well lighted for nocturnal boat launching and her car was parked down by the ramp. She must have come in by the other road.

I had closed the gap and she abandoned the idea of the car, too much time to get in and start up, and ran down to the pier, face contorted, brandishing the needle still. She was still spouting psych jargon. Maybe she was going for the boat although I thought that bad tactics since it would take longer to start and she wasn't getting my boat.

She made the turn around the first piling, took two giant steps on the pier, and went through a hole.

I was on her in a flash. Burning in my back. I could feel the first floaty effects of the shot beginning to break through my rush. But I tried to shrug it off, mind over matter, power of the will, whatever. I bent down to her unmoving figure.

Her right hand was underneath her body and one leg was stuck down through the hole in the pier and I winced, thinking of the rough cedar scraping the soft flesh on the inside of her thighs. I extracted her semigently and rolled her over and the hand rolled free, leaving the long needle embedded in the left side of her stomach. Winstons floated in the slip.

Talk about hari-kari, I thought woozily, and turned to face Evans, who came lumbering up spouting questions and curses. He was highly agitated and I turned to placate him and said, "Gonwarp!"

Then I fell face-first into the water and mud. Again.

40

I WAS SURPRISED TO wake up. Then I giggled, remembering my pratfall. The smart-ass kid at the bait camp would never let me forget it. Twice! I giggled to myself. Bet Melissa was surprised too, and Evans.

Sure was dark.

Gradually I opened my eyes, giggling because that's why I thought it was dark, wonder how I could forget something so simple, must be getting old.

People. Lots of people. Uniforms. John Orton was there, looking official. Other uniforms. Guy in a dark suit, seemed to be the leader, at least he was talking. Better when it was dark, so I closed my eyes.

They were speaking to me. Clanking and whirring from somewhere and I felt the head of the bed elevate. Wonder what your average hospital bed costs, with all the electric motors, seems comfortable enough. Had to pee.

I croaked something, realizing that somebody had poured Elmer's white glue in my throat. Tried the eyes again. Went to rub them and my hand hurt because there was a needle in it. Probably Melissa. Melissa and her damn needles. Girl could flat catch a tarpon though.

Gradually the questions came through and I realized I was in a hospital, must be Port Lavaca hospital because I was on the ground floor and always I had been higher in other hospitals. I could see out a window, patch of grass, ground level, must be Port Lavaca. I didn't remember getting here and the guy in the suit was repeating himself. Bad manners, give me a chance, will you? Evans was back in the back and I tried to wave to him, hurting my hand from the needle again. Hate needles. Hospitals all smell the same, small or large.

Somebody bustled in, black lady in white uniform, open up, thermometer, check the eyelids, mess with my needle hand, blood pressure. I closed my eyes.

Everything was coming back in a rush and the guy in the suit, nice suit, realized the problem and gave me a sip of tepid water through a bent straw, clever idea to corrugate the straw so as to let it bend and I could croak pretty good. Questions.

I closed my eyes and drifted away. Easier.

Some hours later I was awake and had the world's ultimate hangover and answered questions until I was blue in the face. The IV was gone from my hand and I had a green glob taste in my mouth. Yes I had waited for Melissa, yes there was a fight, yes I had hit the guy, Horce, with the cast net and chased her, no I didn't know what was in the needle, yes I had worked for Melissa's clinic, and yes I had had problems with her before. Then they got serious. No mention of Dear Don Nelson, Melissa's financial backer. Probably had his tracks well covered.

We went over the demise of Dr. Natelson five times by my count and I forgot to count the first couple of times. Man, I was hungry. Finally most of them left, Sheriff Orton getting in the last licks, obviously a bit put out because of all the other uniforms on his patch, shaking of head and dire warnings. "Don't like this kind of stuff down here."

Did he suppose I thought it a lark? I made inquiries and found I was in the Victoria hospital, not Port Lavaca, about three blocks from my office and on the ground floor. I got that right, at least.

Evans was left, patiently waiting. He had shook his head at me, looking past several uniforms, when I got a bit testy in my replies and I had mended my ways immediately. Even when they asked the same question several times. The guy in the suit used a gold Cross pen, others tended toward Bic ballpoints.

"You're either the smartest fellow I know or you're so damn lucky I'd like to take you to Vegas," Evans said after all the officials had finally left. Many warnings, cautions, reprimands, suggestions, insider cop comments and muted laughs.

"I know what I'd say," I mumbled.

"In Vegas?"

"Given those two choices. Have they found Kandy? And Tammy, I forgot to ask."

"Both of 'em were at that clinic. Both of them are fine, up to the house. Mamma's with them."

"Good lady."

He gave me a short nod and explained that good ol' Horce had been subdued (thirty-three stitches he said and I was proud in an unseemly fashion) and had told the authorities most of what they wanted to know. "Not so loyal to that lady-doctor after all," said Evans. "When the cops leaned on him."

"How's Melissa . . . Dr. Stone?"

He looked at me for a long time and said, "You don't have to worry about her anymore. You never should have brought her down here, that was wrong."

"How is she?"

He drew his hand across his throat in a slashing gesture. "That shit in the hypo was some sort of nerve something and she never had a chance. The EMS guys were there inside of five minutes, from the fire station? Never had a chance."

"Jesus." I fell back on the bed and considered. Funny how we blank out death, push it away from precious immortal me. Like a bad smell, we want nothing to do with death, go away, don't touch me. I struggled to hold onto memories of Melissa, the good ones, but they skittered out of my mind, shadows and glints mostly.

"They understand she flipped?"

"Yeah. Lots of evidence. Your friend . . . Dr. Edfelter? He was organizing an investigation and when the cops figured out where the witnesses were, they went out there."

"To the clinic."

"Yeah. Both girls were there and they told the same story I just heard you tell."

"About sixteen times."

"Yeah. They even had a guy here from the Food and Drug Administration, can you believe that?"

"Because of her chemicals?"

"Yeah. Seems like she was using stuff that's not even been approved for animal testing. They seemed maddest about that." He shrugged.

"Dr. Natelson would be hurt."

"He's just as dead either way. Looks like you're gonna make it though. The needle just grazed the skin, you got just a touch of that stuff."

"Like you said: lucky."

"Or something. Just what did you have in mind, sitting up there in your house with the shades up, fat, dumb, and happy?"

"I was going to reason with her, Evans, reason with her."

"Yeah," he said. "You ain't planning any more bloodshed, are you? 'Cause if you are, I think we're going to run you out of town. Never had this before."

"Not me. Me and fish, that's it from now on," I said. "Go home. Kiss the girls for me. When do I get out of here? Maybe I'll forgo the fishing, keep my nose in the business." I was hoping he would approve of this thought.

"In some ways, I kinda hope you're stuck right here for a while," he said and left.

41

V<small>INCE CAME BY TO</small> tell me he was borrowing the boat on the day I was getting discharged. No authorities had visited me for a day and nobody said I couldn't leave. Apparently the shrinks had drawn up ranks and divided out the patients from Melissa's clinic. Lots of newspaper coverage, some of it accurate. I was a bit player, thanks be to God. Mostly sex stories about crazy shrink and her insurance scams. Tammy had her picture in the paper, Kandy would be jealous. We may have set mental health back twenty years, not my intent.

Vince had had the prop replaced and the engine ran fine, he said. Told me he was sorry he had missed all the fun but I shouldn't beat up girls, at least fatally. That was Vince's idea of a joke. Business was great at the club, nobody was worrying about being poisoned, and Kandy was quitting dancing altogether, she told him. Finally. Then he left to chase fish.

I pouted because I thought he should have waited for me.

I rang for the weary nurse, the one who couldn't be bothered to hear the punchline of my jokes. Perhaps I needed to work on the old charm some.

"When can I get out of here?" I asked her.

"When the doctor says so."

"Please tell him I'm going to leave AMA if he doesn't hurry up," I told her.

"American Medical Association?"

"Against medical advice."

So they finally let me go and Sheriff Orton had left me a message so I stopped in his office and got some more advice, the gist of which was stop having trouble or he'd bust my head. "Remember the slogan you wrote for me?" he asked. I did, something clever about busting heads legally, and found it not quite so palatable when I was the potential bustee.

Leaving his office in the blinding glare from the late summer sun, I wished I was not so universally thought of as a troublemaker. I fully expected another lecture from Mrs. Evans, and Vince would no doubt have a few choice words of counsel whenever he got back with my boat.

Also I didn't have a car. Nobody seemed concerned about that. Is there anything as lonely as getting out of the hospital and nobody remembers to pick you up? I trudged down the street to my office, plywood and burlap desks, good prints on the wall and a hostile telephone answering machine.

All the urgent calls were old.

My new psychiatric group had apparently given up on me and I wondered if I would collect for the ads I had managed to get placed before Melissa got so radical.

I further wondered just what the hell I would do from this point forward. I wasn't responsible for her death. I looked hard at it, coldly. Sure I had chased her and sure the violence had escalated because of my tricky response to her attacks on me and sure I knew she was on the outer edge of the sanity envelope. Maybe working with disturbed people makes you that way or maybe she had got into working with disturbed people because she was that way.

But I played more-or-less fair, probably more than you should expect from an adperson, and the fall on the pier was an accident. Perhaps the moral is don't have accidents when you're carrying a lethal hypodermic.

Or don't mess with sexy doctors.

Or stay out of other people's computers.

Or—

"There you are," said Tammy from the office door. She had respiked her hair and a wave of maudlin memory swept over me. I hugged her thoroughly, noting in my lecherous old way that her figure was coming back rapidly, hell, was back. Somebody cared. I saw Kandy over her shoulder and adjusted my hug technique.

"I told you," said Kandy. "You look like the kind of guy who gets screwed up over a woman." I released Tammy quickly and hugged up on Kandy. Comparisons are odious but I made them.

"You're probably wondering why I called this meeting," I said happily.

"We've been comparing notes," said Kandy.

I blanched. They both looked extremely, dangerously, content. "I only have one body to offer," I said bravely.

"Poof," said Tammy.

"Looks kinda skinny to me," said Kandy.

"Not much endurance," said Tammy.

"A streak runner, not for the long haul, carrying a load." Kandy grinned.

"Jesus Christ," I said.

"What we think," said Kandy, seriously. "What we think is that we both like to hang around with you now and again but not for the long haul, you know?"

I immediately felt rejected, placed in a nonpermanent category, a person to be trifled with, not worthy of a serious woman for serious matters.

"Hey, gimme a break. I have solid and stable characteristics," I said.

"Most of which are among the missing," said Tammy. "Besides my career demands most of my attention."

"What is your career these days?"

"I'm back to school for my master's and then I'm going into counseling," she said.

While I was trying to digest this, and remember what degree she had at the undergraduate level, Kandy pointed out that she had several thousand dollars saved and was on her way to the West Coast to study commercial art at San Diego State. Everybody was going to boogie and I was in Victoria, Texas, with no clients and few prospects.

"California girls probably can't handle the Texas competition," she said smugly. I doubted that but from somewhere came up with the wisdom not to voice it. Jesus, I thought we had something going, I thought. Neuroses melding together nicely, friends, I did the dishes after she cooked, no major problems, possibility of a good life. *McCall's Magazine* ethic. Why does everybody always bug out on me? Insecurities arose and danced a nasty dance in back of my eyes. I smiled coolly and they saw right through me, much patting and "you'll be okay and it's not forever and don't look so sad." What was I supposed to do, dance a jig? Women are so damn practical.

"So this is good-bye or at least so long," Tammy said. They both had the grace to get a bit teary-eyed and we had much hugging and kissing and keep-in-touch promising and they were off. Counseling? Hell, she was a patient not six months ago. But who would make a better counselor? I reflected.

"You don't happen to have a sister, either one of you?" I asked. They sneered a simultaneous sneer at me and left. I was numb and scared and three years old and it was dark out there.

And I still didn't have a ride. Was I going to have to call a Victoria taxi for the forty-mile trip?

The phone rang and it was Vince from Evans's house and he had just located the largest school of redfish the world has ever known and would I please hurry up and get back to come wadefishing with him?

"I have no girlfriend, no business, no friends, and I just got out of the hospital," I said. "And you want me to come chase redfish when I should be putting my life together. I have a business to rebuild and I don't have a car and I'm all alone and need to think. Redfish! I don't even think I'm going to *try* to catch fish anymore, concentrate on business, settle down, maybe . . . hell, I may get married again or something."

"I'm not believing these fish," he said. "Come *on*, I'll guide you, bait your hook."

The other phone rang and I put him on hold.

"Mr. Beaumont," a rich, cultured voice said. "You're a difficult man to get in contact with."

"I've been tied up recently." I racked my brain over the payables, I thought everything was paid up.

"Obviously, success breeds success," he said. "My name is Dr. Stuart Tomlins and I'm the Medical Director and Administrator for the Stafford Clinic here in Houston. Perhaps you've heard of us?"

I mumbled.

"In any event, we are a full-service, free-standing psychiatric facility and I must tell you we have admired your work, your advertising, enormously. I have the Board of

248 · Peter Barthelme

Regents meeting this afternoon and I wonder, realizing this is short notice but I've been trying to get in touch with you for days, if you might come discuss our marketing with them. It must be this afternoon but you'll find us receptive to any reasonable arrangement. I also think you'll find the budget figures quite . . . substantial. We plan on marketing this facility like no other psychiatric facility has ever been marketed. We've talked to several firms and we really have decided on you, but the board will be here only for a short time. I'm sorry about the short notice, again. There are enormous profit potentials, if one uses all the tools of modern marketing to the fullest extent—"

"Just a moment," I said into the phone, and put him on hold. Then I punched the other line back up.

"Vince," I said. "Can you get here in thirty minutes?"